PROJECT:
Run Away

JF
Carlson, Melody.
Project: Run away

MID-CONTINENT PUBLIC LIBRARY
Parkville Branch
8815 N.W. 45 Highway
Parkville, MO 64152
PV

WITHDRAWN
FROM THE RECORDS OF THE
MID-CONTINENT PUBLIC LIBRARY

Other books in the growing Faithgirlz!™ series

The Faithgirlz!™ Bible
NIV Faithgirlz!™ Backpack Bible
My Faithgirlz!™ Journal

Introducing a new Faithgirlz!™ series from Melody Carlson:

Girls of 622 Harbor View
Project: Girl Power (Book One)
Project: Mystery Bus (Book Two)
Project: Rescue Chelsea (Book Three)
Project: Take Charge (Book Four)
Project: Raising Faith (Book Five)

Other books by Melody Carlson:

Diary of a Teenage Girl Series
TrueColors Series
Degrees Series
Piercing Proverbs
ByDesign Series Nonfiction

Check out www.faithgirlz.com

the beauty of believing

PROJECT:
Run Away

Melody Carlson

ZONDERVAN.com/
AUTHORTRACKER
follow your favorite authors

MID-CONTINENT PUBLIC LIBRARY
Parkville Branch
8815 N.W. 45 Highway
Parkville, MO 64152
PV

MID-CONTINENT PUBLIC LIBRARY - BTM

3 0003 00626790 8

Project: Run Away
Copyright © 2008 by Melody Carlson

Requests for information should be addressed to:
Zonderkidz, *Grand Rapids, Michigan* 49530

Library of Congress Cataloging-in-Publication Data

Carlson, Melody.-
    Project : run away / by Melody Carlson.
       p. cm. -- (Girls of 622 Harbor view ; bk.6)
    Summary: When her mother's abusive ex-husband returns and Emily and her mother flee Oregon,
Emily's friends in the 622 Harbor View Club pray for her and devise a rescue plan to ensure that Emily
and her family return to Oregon.
      ISBN 978-0-310-71350-0 (softcover)
      [1. Clubs--Fiction.   2.Christian life--Fiction.   3. Oregon--Fiction.   ]   I. Title.
PZ7.S6228Hip 2006
{Fic}—dc22

2007044552

All Scripture quotations, unless otherwise indicated, are taken from the HOLY BIBLE, NEW
INTERNATIONAL VERSION®. Copyright © 1973, 1978, 1984 by International Bible Society.
Used by permission of Zondervan. All rights reserved.

All rights reserved. No part of this publication may be reproduced, stored in a retrieval system, or transmitted in any form or by any means—electronic, mechanical, photocopy, record-
ing, or any other—except for brief quotations in printed reviews, without the prior permission
of the publisher.

Zonderkidz is a trademark of Zondervan.

Editor: Barbara Scott
Art direction and design: Merit Alderink
Interior composition: Carlos Eluterio Estrada

Printed in the United States of America

08 09 10 11 12 • 5 4 3 2 1

So we fix our eyes not on what is seen, but what is unseen.
For what is seen is temporary, but what is unseen is eternal.

— 2 Corinthians 4:18

chapter one

"What do you mean I can't go on the ski trip?" Emily asked her mom for the third time. "I earned all my money and I'm all registered and I —"

"It doesn't have to do with any of that," said Mom as she jerked a suitcase from the shelf in her closet, dusted it off, and then tossed it onto her bed.

"And why are you getting that out?" demanded Emily. "Are you going somewhere?"

"We're *all* going somewhere," said Mom. "I want you to go to your room and pack."

"Are we going somewhere for Christmas?" asked Emily, still confused. It was less than a week before Christmas, and this was the first she'd heard of a trip.

"Something like that," said Mom quickly. "Just do as I say and I'll explain later."

"But what about Kyle?" asked Emily. "Isn't he going too?"

"Yes. I'll have to pack for him. He's still at work. We'll pick him up on our way out."

"What am I supposed to pack?" asked Emily, hoping that they might be going somewhere fun.

"Everything," said Mom as she pulled open a drawer.

"What do you mean *everything?*"

"I mean everything that you brought when we moved here last spring. And anything you bought since then. Don't pack any of the things that Morgan's family loaned us. Those will have to be returned ... later."

"*Returned?*"

"Oh, Emily," said Mom in her exasperated voice as she tossed a handful of socks and underclothes into her bag. "I don't have time for questions right now. We need to get moving — and out of here — fast!"

Emily stared at her mom in horror. "Are we leaving — I mean moving — for good?"

"I'm sorry, Emily. I wish it wasn't true."

"But ... but ... why?" Emily felt a lump like a hard rock growing in her throat.

"It's your father ..."

"Dad?"

"Yes ..." Mom stood up straight and, pushing a strand of blonde hair from her eyes, she looked at Emily with an expression that Emily remembered from back in the old days, back before they moved to Boscoe Bay. "I just found out that he knows where we are."

"How would he know? How did you find that out?"

"I just happened to call your Aunt Becky this morning. I used a friend's cell phone at work, so it couldn't be traced back … I just wanted to wish her a Merry Christmas." Mom carried a bunch of clothes from her closet and tossed them onto the already crowded bed. "Becky told me that your dad hired a private investigator who somehow tracked us down. She said that he is on his way here right now. So, don't you see, Emily? We have to get out of here — immediately!"

"But why do *we* have to be the ones to run away?" pleaded Emily. "We haven't done anything wrong!"

"I know." Mom sighed loudly.

"He's the one who should be running, Mom. He's the one who's done all the bad stuff."

"I know … I know …" Mom sighed loudly. "There's no time to talk about this now. Just go pack, Emily. Hurry."

"But, Mom!" Emily pleaded with her. "I have friends here. I have a life and I don't want to — "

"Neither do I, Emily. But it's what we *have* to do. I told you and Kyle, right from the start, that our stay in Boscoe Bay might be brief."

"But what does that mean, Mom?" asked Emily in desperation. "That we'll have to keep running and running forever?"

"I don't know …" Mom closed her eyes and shook her head. "All I know is that we need to get out of here right *now.*" She narrowed her eyes and gave Emily a look that said "I am dead serious, and I want no argument."

"Okay," said Emily as she went to her room. Tears were filling her eyes as she began to gather her things and pile them on the futon bed that Morgan had loaned to her when they first came here. It was funny … she'd come to think of that bed, as well as so many other things, as her own. Suddenly it seemed as if nothing was really hers. Not her home or her school … and worst of all, not her friends.

"Here," said Mom after a few minutes. "Just stuff your things into these." She tossed several large black trash bags into Emily's bedroom. "I'm going to pack for Kyle now."

Before long, Emily was done, but Mom was still gathering things up. "Can I go tell Morgan that I'm leaving?" Emily asked sadly.

Mom frowned. "I don't know …"

"But they're going to wonder what happened to us," Emily persisted. "We were supposed to go to their house for Christmas. And I was supposed to meet the girls at the clubhouse this afternoon. They might think we've been abducted or something. And, knowing Morgan, she might even call the police."

Mom nodded. "Yes. You're right. They've been good friends to us. And we can trust them. Go ahead and tell them that we're leaving this afternoon. I've already explained things to Mr. Greeley. Tell Mrs. Evans that Mr. Greeley can give her the house key so that they can come collect their — their things." Mom's voice broke and tears came streaming down her cheeks now.

"Oh, Mom," said Emily, running over to hug her. "This is so horrible."

"I know," said Mom as she ran her hand over Emily's hair. "I wish there was another way."

"Why isn't there?" asked Emily.

Mom just shook her head. "I don't know …" Then Mom turned back to packing Kyle's things.

"I'm going to Morgan's," said Emily as she grabbed her jacket.

"Don't stay long," warned Mom. "I'm almost ready to go right now, and if you don't get back here in time, I'll just drive over there and honk — and you better come a-running."

"Okay."

Emily picked up Morgan's Christmas present. It wasn't much, just a leopard-print picture frame with a photo of her and Morgan in it. The gift wasn't even wrapped, but Emily didn't want to miss the chance to give it to her. Also, she'd have to ask Morgan to give the gifts (the things she and Morgan had been working on the past few days) to their other friends for her.

"Hey, Em," said Morgan happily as she opened the door. "I'm so glad you're here. I've got something I want to show you."

Emily stepped into Morgan's living room as Morgan dashed off toward her bedroom. Emily looked around the cozy house, trying to memorize every single thing about this place in one quick glance. The happy clutter of Grandma's homemade afghans and worn furniture mixed with the more eclectic style of Morgan's mom's art and nicer things. From the first time Emily had stepped through their front door, she had always felt welcome here.

"Hello, Emily," called Grandma from her recliner.

"How are you feeling today?" asked Emily as she approached her. Morgan's grandma had recently undergone some very serious heart surgery and had only been sitting up for a few days now.

"I'm feeling right as rain," said Grandma.

"I'm glad." Emily forced a smile as she looked down at her.

Grandma frowned. "But what about you, honey? You don't look too well to me."

"Oh, I'm a little sad," said Emily. *What an understatement.*

"*Sad?*" Grandma peered curiously at her. "Whatever for?"

"Yeah?" said Morgan as she reappeared wearing an interesting hat that appeared to have been patchworked together from scraps of polar fleece — probably the leftovers from her recent sock-sewing project. "What's up, Em?"

Emily tried to blink back the tears, but it was impossible. "We have to … have to leave."

Morgan frowned. "You mean you guys are going somewhere for Christmas? I thought you were going to come to our house for —"

"No, I mean, I mean we have to leave … for … for good!" Now Emily was crying full force.

"Why?" cried Morgan, running over and putting her arms around Emily.

"Yes, why?" said Grandma more calmly.

Emily worked hard to recover from her outburst, finally taking a tissue from Grandma's hand. "Thanks."

"Now, sit down on the sofa there and tell us exactly what's going on," Grandma commanded her.

"Well..." Emily took in a slow breath. "You know a little bit about why we came here. You guys and Mr. Greeley are the only ones who know about..."

"You mean about your father?" supplied Grandma.

"Yes." Emily nodded. "I guess he's found out where we are."

"So?" said Morgan in a defiant tone. It was actually sort of how Emily felt herself when Mom first told her the news.

"So... my mom says that means we have to go."

"But why?" demanded Morgan. Her dark eyes were filling with tears too.

"I don't really know..." Emily looked down at her hands in her lap. "I guess it's because Mom thinks he might hurt us again."

"But how can he hurt you?" asked Morgan. "I mean what about police protection and things like that?"

"I don't know..." Emily just shook her head.

"Morgan does have a point," said Grandma. "Running away might not solve your problem, Emily. Sometimes it's better to stay and fight for your rights. You and your family have good friends here in the mobile-home park, as well as at church. You have a community that could stand behind you and protect you. If you're out someplace new, where people don't know you … well, that might be less safe."

Emily looked up at Grandma's kind brown face and nodded. "Yes, yes … that makes sense."

"It does," said Morgan. "I mean, what if you guys were out on the road, staying at a hotel or something, and your dad found you there? Which would be worse?"

Emily considered this. "I know what you mean." Then she thought of her mother. "But for some reason Mom doesn't see it that way."

"But *why?*" cried Morgan. "It just seems so wrong that your family should have to be on the run from your dad. *Why? Why? Why?*"

Just then, Emily heard Mom's car horn honking out front. "I've got to go," she said quickly. "Mom said to tell you that Mr. Greeley has the key to our house and you guys can go over there whenever you want to get your things." She held out her gift for Morgan. "This was going to be your Christmas present." Again came the honking sound. "I didn't have time to wrap it."

"But, Emily —"

"I've got to go," said Emily.

"I'm not even done with your present yet," said Morgan. Then she pulled the brightly colored hat from her head and shoved it onto Emily's head. "Here, take this for now." Then she hugged her again. "I don't want you to leave."

"I don't want to leave."

"You're my best friend ever," cried Morgan.

"You're mine too!" sobbed Emily.

This time Mom's horn honked loud and long.

"You better go, honey," said Grandma. "But please tell your mom what we said. And if there is anything we can do — I mean anything at all — please, call us. Remember you have your friends, the church, the community here ... there's a lot of power in those kinds of numbers."

"I'll tell Mom." Emily ran over and quickly hugged Grandma. "Thanks ... for everything."

"You be sure and call us, Emily," said Grandma. "And you can call collect if you need to. And don't forget that wherever you go God is with you. And we are praying for you."

"Yes," said Morgan. "And this isn't over yet. I'm going to pray for God to bring you back here to us, Emily."

"We'll all be praying for that," called Grandma.

Emily thanked them again, then went out the door just as Mom began to honk the horn one more time. It was starting to rain as Emily ran out to the car. She wished that what Morgan and Grandma were saying could really be true — she wished it was possible for them to pray her and her family back here to Harbor View. But as she got into the car, she couldn't forget the last time their family had to run, leaving their home and everything behind. They never did go back then. Why would this time be any different?

chapter two

"We have an emergency," said Morgan when all the girls were finally seated in the clubhouse.

"Where's Emily?" asked Chelsea.

"Exactly," said Morgan. "That's the emergency."

"Did she get hurt?" asked Amy.

"No." Then, since there seemed to be no reason to keep this thing secret any longer, Morgan explained why Emily's family had to flee so suddenly this afternoon.

"Wow," said Chelsea. "I had no idea."

"Poor Emily," said Carlie.

"That's crazy," said Amy. "Why should Emily's family have to run away from a dad who treated them like that?"

"That's what I think too," said Morgan.

"They need a lawyer," said Chelsea.

"I'm sure they can't afford one," said Morgan.

"My dad has a friend who's a lawyer," said Chelsea. "In fact, Emily babysat for them to earn money for the ski trip."

"This means Emily is going to miss the ski trip," said Amy sadly.

"Not if we can help them," said Morgan.

"How can we help them?" asked Carlie.

"Do we even know how to reach them?" asked Chelsea.

Morgan considered this. "Not really."

"Then how can we help them?" asked Amy.

"By praying," said Morgan. "We'll start by praying."

So, right then and there, all four girls bowed their heads and prayed for Emily and her family. They prayed for God to protect them and to get them safely back to Boscoe Bay and Harbor View.

"Amen," said Morgan when they'd finished.

The girls sat quietly in the bus for about a minute. All they could hear was the sound of the Oregon rain beating down on the roof of the bus.

"So, I guess this means our Christmas party is off," said Amy sadly.

"I know I don't feel much like a party," said Morgan.

"Me neither," added Carlie.

"I'm calling my dad," said Chelsea as she opened up her cell phone.

"Why?" asked Morgan.

"I'm going to ask him to talk to Mr. Lawrence. He's a lawyer, and Dad can ask him if he can figure out a way to help Emily's family."

"Great," said Morgan.

"But even if Mr. Lawrence is willing to help them … how do we let Emily's mom know about it?" asked Amy.

"Yeah," said Carlie, "it seems pretty impossible."

"I guess we'll just have to keep praying," said Morgan. "Because God is the only one I know who can do what's impossible."

"And we'll do whatever we can to help," said Carlie.

Morgan held up her arm with the rainbows rule bracelet. "All for one, and one for all?"

The other girls, including Chelsea — who was talking to her dad now — held up their arms in unison.

"I know, Daddy," said Chelsea. "But this *is* an emergency." Then she told him about Emily's situation, painting a dramatic account of how Emily's family was, right this minute, fleeing in fear for their own safety. Chelsea listened for a minute or two. "Yes," she said with excitement. "That's exactly what I thought too. They need a lawyer. What about Mr. Lawrence?" She waited again. "You will, Daddy?" She smiled happily at her friends now. "Thanks so much! Yes, I'll leave my phone on. Thank you, Daddy!" Then she closed her phone.

"Is he going to talk to the lawyer?"

"Yep."

"But, even if he talks to the lawyer," Amy reminded them, "we don't know how to reach Emily right now."

"That's why we have to keep praying," said Morgan.

They called their meeting to a close earlier than usual, and all of them promised to keep praying for Emily.

"Can I stay at your house until my mom gets here?" Chelsea asked Morgan as they started trudging down the wet sandy trail back to the mobile-home park.

"Sure," said Morgan.

Although it was still raining, all four girls paused briefly in front of Emily's now abandoned house. They just stood there looking sadly at it.

"This isn't over yet," proclaimed Morgan.

Now Chelsea stuck her hand with the bracelet on it in the air. "Here's to rescuing Emily," she said.

"To rescuing Emily," echoed Morgan, and the others joined in. Then they ran off to their houses.

Once Morgan and Chelsea were inside the house, and before they even removed their wet jackets, Chelsea was calling her mom to ask her to pick her up. "We quit early," she told her, explaining about Emily's family's unexpected departure. "Daddy is calling Mr. Lawrence right now," she said. "We're all going to do whatever we can to get Emily back here."

"Excuse me for eavesdropping," said Grandma as the girls came into the living room. "But who is Mr. Lawrence?"

Morgan told Grandma about Chelsea's idea, and Grandma smiled. "Yes," she said. "That's exactly how a community should work. People helping one another."

"Do you want a Christmas cookie?" asked Morgan. "Emily and I decorated them just the other day."

"Sure," said Chelsea, following Morgan into the kitchen.

"Want some too?" Morgan called out to Grandma. "And some tea?"

Soon the three of them were back in the living room having cookies and tea and discussing ways they might be able to find out where Emily's family was.

"You have to give your license plate numbers when you stay at a hotel," Chelsea said between bites. "I know, because my mom never can remember hers, and I usually have to run out and check."

"But we don't know Emily's mom's license number," said Morgan. "At least I don't."

"Me neither," said Chelsea. "Do you have any idea which way they were going? North, south, east, or west?"

"Not west," said Morgan. "That would be straight into the Pacific Ocean."

"And I doubt they're going east," said Chelsea, "if they originally ran away from Idaho like you said."

"My guess is south," said Grandma as she set her teacup down.

"Why?" asked Morgan.

"A couple of reasons ... one, it's warmer down there in the winter time, and two, there are more people down in California, it's probably easier to disappear."

"That's true," said Chelsea. "It's a lot more crowded down there than up here."

"We need a map," said Morgan suddenly. "A road map."

"There's one in my car," said Grandma. "In the glove compartment."

So Morgan dashed out to the carport and returned with a map, which she soon had spread across the coffee table. "So," she began, "if they're going south, they might be on this highway right here." She looked at the clock. "They left almost two hours ago." She glanced at Grandma. "How fast do you think they're driving on this highway?"

"Not more than sixty miles an hour," said Grandma. "That's a curvy road, and the weather isn't very good for driving."

Morgan checked the key on the map and did some quick figuring. "Well, Emily's mom still had to pick up Kyle, so that used up some time. So if they've been on the road for, say, an hour and a half, maybe that means they're about here by now."

"Hey, that's pretty good," said Chelsea. "Do you really think so?"

Morgan shrugged. "If Grandma is right and they're really going south."

Just then, they heard a horn honking. Morgan jumped to her feet, dashing to the window, thinking that it was Emily's mom again. But it was just Mrs. Landers in her Mercedes. "Your mom is here," Morgan called back to Chelsea.

Chelsea tugged on her still-wet parka.

"Well, let's keep in touch," said Chelsea. "We need to do everything we can to get Emily back here."

"And let's keep praying," Morgan reminded her.

"Absolutely," said Chelsea. Then Chelsea did something that Morgan couldn't ever remember her doing before. She reached out and hugged Morgan. "I'm glad we're friends, Morgan."

Morgan nodded. "Me too."

"And somehow we're going to get Emily back here."

"See ya," called Morgan as Chelsea dashed out into the rain.

Morgan closed the door and went back to where Grandma was just finishing up her tea. "Chelsea seems like a nice girl," said Grandma.

"Yeah," agreed Morgan. "I've had my doubts sometimes, but I think you're right. She really is a nice girl."

Grandma chuckled. "I suppose that some people can be just as prejudiced against rich people as others are prejudiced against black people."

Morgan sighed. "Yeah, I suppose so."

"Aren't you glad that God sees past all that?"

"That's for sure," said Morgan as she cleaned up the tea things.

"Well, I suppose I should go have a little rest," said Grandma.

"Need any help?" offered Morgan.

"No, honey, I'm fine. I feel stronger every day."

Morgan thought about Emily as she rinsed off the plates and cups in the kitchen sink. She wondered if her calculations about their road trip were even close. Was Emily's car really about a hundred miles south of Boscoe Bay right now? Were they still driving along the Oregon coast highway, wipers slapping against the windshield so that they could see their way through this rain? She wondered how Emily and her brother were feeling just now. Were they all talking? Or was the car silent and somber? She imagined the three of them packed in there between all their personal belongings. Was it cramped? Surely Emily must feel as if her whole life had just been jerked out from under her — all over again. Her family would have to relocate, get started in new schools, get new jobs. It was overwhelming for Morgan to even try to wrap her head around it. And what about Christmas, which was less than a week away? Where would they be by then? In some shabby motel room? Morgan couldn't imagine how she would feel if she were in Emily's shoes. Poor Emily!

Out of habit, Morgan reached up to finger one of her beaded braids. It was something she did when she was feeling anxious about something. And then she would pray about whatever was bothering her. But, as she touched a soft curl, she remembered that the beaded braids were gone, and she instantly wished that she'd never gotten her hair changed. What had she been thinking? Of course, she knew exactly what she'd been thinking. She'd been jealous of the developing friendship between Emily and Chelsea. She had wanted to look less her African-American self and more like them. How totally stupid! And now Emily was gone and Morgan actually was starting to like Chelsea much better. Grandma was right. Morgan had been wrong about Chelsea. Funny how life could change like that — so quickly.

As Morgan stood there, she was looking directly across the road at Mr. Greeley's house. Suddenly she remembered something that Emily had said about Mr. Greeley, about him knowing that Emily's family was leaving and having a key to their house so they could pick up their things. Well, some of the things at Emily's belonged to Morgan — although, in her heart, she had given them to Emily. Still, it provided a good excuse to go snoop around. And maybe she could uncover something that would help them locate Emily. Something that could help bring Emily and her family back here — back where they belonged!

chapter three

No one spoke in the car for quite awhile. Emily knew that they were all feeling very sad about leaving Boscoe Bay. Kyle had put up a lot of protest when Mom picked him up at the gas station where he'd been working these past few months. Kyle even suggested that he might stay behind and live with a friend, but Mom wouldn't hear of it. Mom had told him that he didn't understand the problems of child custody laws. And even when Emily tried to chime in, Mom had shut her down. Mom said she didn't want to hear a single word from either of them right then, that she needed them to be quiet so she could focus on driving safely and so she could figure out what their next move might be.

For the next hour, Emily wrote in her journal. She wrote and wrote and wrote. And as she wrote, she remembered a book she'd just read. She'd picked it out just before Christmas break from the recommended reading list from her English class. Morgan had thought the book looked boring, but the story had really gotten to Emily. In fact, she wished she'd brought it with her because she thought she'd like to read it again.

It was called *Anne Frank: The Diary of a Young Girl.* The girl in the book, Anne, had been a real person. And, like Emily, she had written in a diary about her life. And, like Emily, Anne had been thirteen. And she had been faced with a frightening dilemma. But Anne's troubles were far worse than Emily's. And by the time Emily finished the book, which in Emily's opinion was too short, she decided that Anne Frank was one of the bravest people she had ever read about. And for some reason this gave Emily a bit of hope.

If Anne Frank could be brave when all looked hopeless, so could Emily. Besides, Emily reminded herself, she had God. That was something that Anne had struggled with a lot. Emily wanted to go back in time and tell Anne that God really was real and that she should trust him more. Maybe Anne did eventually ... before she died in the concentration camp.

And that's when Emily really began to pray. She begged God to turn this thing around ... and to get them safely back to Boscoe Bay. She wanted to have as much faith as Morgan and Grandma right now. But as their car kept driving about sixty miles an hour due south, it wasn't easy.

"I'm sorry if I sounded grouchy," Mom said finally. "It's just that I am really stressed over this. It wasn't what I wanted either."

"But I don't see why we have to be the ones on the run," said Kyle from the passenger seat in front. "Dad's the one who messed up. He should be running ... from the law."

"It has to do with taking you kids across the state line," Mom explained. "Your dad used to warn me that if I ever ran, if I ever took you guys out of Idaho, he would hire a lawyer and get full custody. Do you know what that means?"

"That we'd have to live with dad?" said Kyle.

"Yes," Mom said with a sigh. "I know I should've done it differently, but I felt so desperate at the time. I just wanted to get away. I saw the chance and I took it."

"And I'm glad you did, Mom," said Emily from the backseat. "It was the right thing to do."

"It seemed right," agreed Mom. "But according to the law, it was wrong."

"Do you know that for sure?" asked Kyle.

"I know that your dad is your parent, as much as I am," said Mom. "And that means he has the right to accuse me of kidnapping—"

"Kidnapping?" cried Emily. "That is perfectly ridiculous. You know that we wanted to come with you, Mom. We hated how Dad treated you. He should be in jail!"

"Yes, I know," said Mom. "But sometimes the law doesn't work like that."

"Well, then the law is wrong," said Kyle.

"As soon as we get settled," said Mom, "and as soon as I can afford it, I will contact a lawyer. I was about to do that back in Boscoe Bay. I even had the name of a guy in town ...

but then this happened. I just never really thought your father would find us. I don't even see how he did. Especially after we changed our last name. I switched cars ... I thought I did everything I could."

"Do you think it was from those two times my friends and I were photographed and in the newspaper?" asked Emily in a weak voice.

"I don't know ..."

"It's such a small paper," said Kyle. "I don't see how."

Even so, Emily felt guilty. She hated to think that their problems were all her fault. She should've been more careful. But after getting settled into Boscoe Bay, after making new friends, she probably had let her guard down. She should've known that Dad wouldn't give up that easily on his family. He was a stubborn and proud man, and she should've known that he would do whatever it took to find them.

Emily had always been afraid of her dad. He had never actually hit her, not like he hit her mother or Kyle, but he had yelled at her and carried on to the point where Emily felt it was likely she'd be next. She had even tried to talk to someone about it once. She had trusted Aunt Becky. But Aunt Becky, just like everyone else, couldn't believe that Emily's dad would ever do anything like that. No one could imagine the rages that he could go into when things didn't go his way. He managed to keep up an image of such a nice guy when he was out

in public. In fact, that was one of the things that would set
him off. He didn't want anyone to mess up his perfect image.
And he couldn't stand it when anyone in his family, whether
it was Kyle or Mom or Emily, did anything that he felt was
"inappropriate behavior." Dad loved the phrase *inappropriate
behavior*. He had a whole list of things that could fall into that
category. Emily wrote them down in her journal.

* Being disrespectful of Dad
  (It was okay to be disrespectful of Mom as long as
  it wasn't in public.)

* Not having perfect manners
  (It reflected poorly on Dad.)

* Wearing unclean or wrinkled clothing
  (It reflected poorly on their family.)

* Using bad grammar
  (although Dad sometimes did without knowing it)

* Getting a bad grade or in trouble at school
  (Kyle got caught skipping in middle school, and
  you would've thought he'd murdered someone.)

* Being late, not doing your chores, not standing up
  straight ...

Emily knew she could make the list longer if she thought
hard enough, but she was tired of thinking about Dad. She

wasn't sure if she actually hated him — and she knew that was probably wrong — but she did know that she didn't want to see him again, and she didn't want to remember how it had been living in the same house with him. And even though they had nicer things and more money then, Emily would never choose to go back to that kind of life. She had never felt comfortable in her home. And she had never wanted to have friends over. She had seen Dad tear into Kyle in front of a friend once, and she had never wanted that to happen to her. As a result, she didn't have many close friends. For sure, she'd never had anyone like Morgan to hang with. This was so unfair.

"Mom," said Emily in a timid voice. "I was just thinking about something that Morgan's grandma told me."

"What's that?"

"Well, she said that it might be safer for you — and for us — to stay in Boscoe Bay."

"Why would it be safer? Can you imagine what would happen if your dad found us?" Mom shook her head. "He would probably show up with the police, accuse me of kidnapping you two ... and for all I know they would take you away and throw me in jail. How would that be safer?"

"That's so wrong," said Kyle as he hit his fist into the dashboard.

"Morgan's grandma said that we have a *community* in Boscoe Bay. She said we have friends who will stand up for us and help. We have our friends in Harbor View and friends at church. She said that we would be safer there than out here on our own. I mean, think about it, Mom, what would we do if Dad found us out here on the road or staying at some motel? We wouldn't have anyone to turn to."

"I'm sure that sounds sensible to Morgan's grandma," said Mom. "But she does not know your father. She doesn't know what that man is capable of. He can be very convincing. I tried before to tell people what he did … don't you remember what happened after that?"

"But you still have those photos I took of you, don't you?" asked Kyle. "That's proof of Dad's abuse. And Boscoe Bay is different than where we lived before. The people there don't know Dad. But they do know us."

"That's right," agreed Emily. "We might have a chance back in Boscoe Bay."

"But what about the law?" asked Mom. "Sure, we might have friends and all that, but what happens when the law says that taking you kids away from your father was wrong? What happens when he has the legal right to take you back and to put me in jail? What then?"

The car got silent again. Emily wanted to ask Mom if she knew these things for certain, if she had really looked into it, or if she was just believing things that Dad had told her — things that he used to frighten her. Emily could remember other times when Dad would scare Mom into seeing things his way. He would use his power to hurt and control her — and sometimes it seemed that Mom wasn't really thinking straight. Was this turning into one of those times?

"I'm hungry," said Emily. "I didn't have any lunch and I — "

"I'm hungry too," said Kyle. "Can we stop and get something in the next town?"

"And I need to use a restroom," added Emily. But what she was thinking was she wanted to find a pay phone. She wanted to call Morgan's grandma and get some more advice.

"Okay, we'll find a fast-food place," said Mom. "And we'll order something to eat in the car. My plan is to drive until we get out of Oregon. Then we'll find a motel in some little town in northern California. But that's as far as I've planned so far."

After about twenty minutes they came to a town, and Mom drove until Kyle spotted a McDonald's. Emily told Mom what she wanted, and then pretending to go to the restroom, she went to the pay phone instead, placing a collect call to Morgan's house.

"Hello?" said Morgan's grandma.

"Grandma," said Emily happily, remembering how she had invited Emily to call her that the very first day they'd met.

"Oh, Emily, honey, how *are* you?"

"Okay, I guess."

"*Where* are you?"

Emily told her. Then she told her about her mom's plan about getting past the state line and staying in the first small town in California. "I'm not even sure where, exactly, but I'll try to call from there."

"Can't you ask your mother to come back?"

"I so wish!" Emily said quickly. "This is the deal, Grandma. My mom is so scared of my dad that she's just really freaked. And I don't think she's really thought this whole thing through, you know what I mean?"

"I understand, Emily … but you should know that your friend Chelsea was here a while ago," said Grandma. "And her father is contacting a lawyer friend — a Mr. Lawrence, I believe — and he may want to help your mom."

"I babysat for him," said Emily as she remembered earning money for the ski trip, the ski trip that she was going to miss now. "He's a nice guy."

"So, perhaps you should give Chelsea a call, dear."

"Okay. I'll do that."

"And, remember, we all want to help you and your family. Tell your mother she has good friends here, folks who will do what they can to help her. And tell her, Emily, that there must be a way to work this thing out without you poor kids always being on the run. God has better answers."

"I'll try to make her see that." Emily thanked Grandma now and hung up, immediately placing a collect call to Chelsea's cell phone and hoping that Chelsea would accept the charges.

"Emily!" cried Chelsea. "Is it really you?"

"Yeah, and I have to talk fast. Mom'll get mad if she finds out what I'm doing. I just talked to Morgan's grandma and she said that Mr. Lawrence might be able to —"

"Yes! He wants to help your mom, Emily. He's doing some legal research right now. Can you call back at my house in a little while?"

"I don't think so … we have to keep driving. But when we stop for the night, at a motel, I'll try to call again. Can I call collect at your house?"

"Of course!"

"I gotta go," said Emily as she noticed her mom's car waiting past the drive-in window now.

"Take care," said Chelsea. "We're all here for you, Emily. We love you, and we're really praying for you."

"Thanks." Then Emily hung up and, without even using the restroom, she dashed back out to the car.

"That took a while," said Emily's mom.

"There was a line," said Emily. And that was true. There was a line. It was just that Emily had not been in the line. Of course, now that they were on the road again, she wished that she had been.

chapter four

"Thanks," said Morgan as Mr. Greeley handed over the key to Emily's house. "I sure do wish the Adams hadn't left like that ..."

"You and me both, Morgan." He shook his head sadly. "Just don't seem right."

"Well, my friends and I are doing everything we can to help them to come back to Boscoe Bay — back where they belong."

Mr. Greeley almost smiled now. "Well, if anyone can make something like that happen, I'd wager it would be you and your friends, Morgan."

"And God," said Morgan. "We need his help."

"You let me know if I can be of any help too. If there's anything I can do, you just let me know. I care about that little family."

"I know you do," said Morgan. She suddenly remembered how it had been Emily who had broken through to Mr. Greeley. It had been Emily who had solved the mystery of Mr. Greeley's estranged son and told him about it. Of course, he would have a special place for Emily in his heart. For that matter, so did Morgan. They had to get her back here!

"Well, I better get going," said Morgan. "Thanks again."

Then she took off running through the rain, trying not to get drenched before she got to Emily's house. Even though it wasn't yet five o'clock, it was dark out. And not a single light was on in the Adams' house. Morgan fumbled in the darkness, trying to get the key into the door as rain dripped down her back. Finally she got it unlocked, opened the door, went in, and turned on the lights, both inside and out. That was much better. Much friendlier. She could almost make herself believe that Emily and her family hadn't really left. Or that they would be home shortly.

She walked through the living room, wondering what it was she was really looking for. She knew she needed some sort of clue ... something to show her where Emily and her family were headed, some way that Morgan and the rest of her friends could locate them and help them. The living room looked much the same as it had when Emily was still here. The same furnishings and things that Morgan's mom had loaned and given them were there, along with some of the things that Emily's mom had purchased later.

Morgan was somewhat surprised to see that the TV was still there, since Emily's mom had worked hard to save for and buy it. But then it was probably too bulky to put in their car, along with all their other belongings. Maybe Morgan's mom could put it in their storage shed for them, to save for them when they came back … if they came back.

Morgan swallowed against the lump that was growing in her throat. Maybe Emily wasn't coming back. Maybe Morgan was just on a wild goose chase right now. She walked around the abandoned house and tried to imagine what it would be like if Emily really was gone for good. Would someone else move into this house? Would Morgan ever hear from Emily again? What if that was it? Was this the end of their friendship?

"No," Morgan said out loud, and her voice echoed in the hallway that led toward the bedrooms. "That's not faith talking." Then she started to pray again. She prayed aloud, asking God to help her to find something in this house that might show her where Emily was and how to reach her. And, once again, she asked God to watch over Emily and her brother and mom. She asked him to work out a way to get them back here. "The sooner the better, dear God," she prayed. "By Christmas would be nice. Thank you. Amen."

Feeling a little more faithful, Morgan walked through the kitchen now. It too looked the same. She looked at the note-pad, even picking it up and holding it on an angle to the light, hoping she might detect some important number or destination. But it looked like a grocery list: milk, eggs, cereal, bread. Nothing that seemed to lead to anything. She looked at the wall phone. It was the old-fashioned kind with a curly cord that kept it attached. If it was like the phone at Grandma's, the one Mom had picked out, Morgan could check the caller ID to see who had called recently. That could provide a good clue. But, as it was, she felt clueless.

She walked down the hallway and peeked in Emily's mom's room. It was messier than usual, with some odd bits and pieces of clothing strewn about, as if someone had packed very quickly. Not enough time to take everything. What if she'd left something behind that she needed? Morgan felt a little guilty for looking through a grown-up's room. It almost seemed like trespassing. And so she continued on. Kyle's room had the same messy look, as if someone had packed recklessly, in a hurry. Morgan pushed a couple of the opened drawers back in, picked up a stray sock and laid it on the dresser, and even straightened his bedspread.

Morgan stood by the door, looking at his room. If you didn't know what was up, all that had gone on today, you might think that the Adams were still living here. All the furnishings were in place. Sports posters still hung on Kyle's wall. Even his football and skateboard were still in the corner, like Kyle would be back any minute.

Finally, Morgan went to Emily's room. She held her breath as she turned on the overhead light. Everything looked almost exactly the same here as well. Emily's bed was neatly made, the colorful plush pillows that she and Morgan had sewn together were lined up along the top, each one in place, all except for the tiger-striped one. That was Emily's favorite and the softest one of the bunch. Hopefully she had that one with her. Morgan pulled open one of Emily's drawers. Empty. The closet was empty too. It seemed that Emily had taken more time to pack. Morgan remembered how little Emily had brought with her when she first moved to Boscoe Bay — literally the clothes on her back. Morgan remembered that day, back when they'd first become friends. Emily had been knocked from her bike by one of the bullies. She'd hurt her knee and torn her jeans. And, later, when Morgan and Emily got better acquainted, Emily confessed that the reason she'd cried wasn't because of her knee, but because she'd torn her jeans — her only jeans. That's when Morgan had mended them and then given her some of the clothes from her own closet, things she still liked, but had outgrown. Emily had been so appreciative. And that was the beginning of a great friendship. A friendship that Morgan wasn't ready to let go of. They needed Emily and her family back here. They needed to stay together!

Morgan picked up a thin paperback book from Emily's dresser. It was one of the books that had been on their recommended reading list in English class, but Morgan had assumed by the rather ordinary-looking cover that it must've been pretty boring. Just a plain black and white photo of a kind of weird-looking girl named Anne Frank. Morgan had actually been surprised when Emily had chosen this book, when it seemed there were so many others that looked far more interesting. But then Emily was really into books — a lot more than Morgan. And Emily often read poetry and old-fashioned books that Morgan had absolutely no interest in.

At least that's what Morgan had thought … until Emily had told her about something she'd just read. Then the book and the characters would seem to come to life, and Morgan would suddenly wonder if she'd missed something. Right now she mostly missed her best friend.

She flipped over the well-worn paperback to read the blurb on the back. The title of the book was *Diary of a Young Girl*, and all that Morgan knew was that it had been written by a girl a long time ago. Back when World War II was going on. Still, Emily had been saying how good it was, and she had teasingly reminded Morgan, "You really shouldn't judge a book by the cover."

Now, as Morgan read the words on the back, she realized that, once again, Emily was probably right. This "boring-looking book" was the story of a thirteen-year-old girl who had hidden with her family in a small attic space to escape persecution from the Nazis during the war. Judging by the blurb, the evil Nazis probably wanted to kill this girl and her family.

Morgan opened the book to the middle, a little trick she'd learned back in grade school, and began to read. And what she read completely surprised her. She actually sat down on Emily's bed and continued to read several pages, getting totally caught up in Anne's story. This teenage girl described the sad conditions of living in a tiny attic with her relatives and not having enough food to eat and having to remain deathly quiet during the daytime. And yet this girl sounded so real and funny and smart. Morgan knew that she would have to read the whole book now, starting from the beginning. Then she and Emily could talk about it. That is if Emily got to come back.

.......Morgan was about to give up when she heard someone knocking. It sounded like the front door. It was probably Mom, home from work and coming to check on her. She'd probably seen the note Morgan had left on the kitchen table, saying she'd come over here to look around. Maybe Mom wanted to help. Or maybe Mom had some kind of news. Feeling suddenly hopeful, Morgan ran through the house to the front door and was just starting to unlock it when the knocking grew intense. It was more like banging than knocking. She paused with her hand frozen on the doorknob. And just then she heard a man's voice shouting loudly.

"Let me in, Lisa! I know you're in there!"

Morgan jerked her hand away from the doorknob, thankful that she had locked it behind her and that it was still locked. Then she stood on tiptoe to peer through the peephole. There, standing under the porch light, was a soggy and angry-faced man. He was swearing and beating on the door like he meant to break it down.

"I can hear you, Lisa!" He yelled. "I know you're there. You better open this door right this minute, or I'm going to kick it in."

With a pounding heart, Morgan slowly backed away from the door. Then she ran to the kitchen and grabbed the phone receiver, immediately dialing her own number, but then wishing she'd called 9-1-1 instead. Too late, Grandma had answered. Her calm, soothing voice seemed out of place with the furious sound of banging and yelling from the direction of the front door.

"Grandma!" said Morgan urgently. "I'm at Emily's house. Someone is trying to break in. Probably Emily's dad. Call the police *right now*. I gotta go!"

Then she hung up the phone, dashed down the hallway, and went straight for Emily's room because it felt the most familiar. But where could she hide? Knowing she couldn't hide beneath the futon bed, she headed for the closet and went inside. She was just closing the door behind her when she heard a loud crash coming from the living room. Morgan shuddered. Emily's dad had broken into the house! And right now, he was stomping through the living room!

Dear God, help me, she prayed silently.

chapter five

The rain finally let up, but it was pitch black out now, and Emily wished that Mom would drive a little slower. Still, she didn't want to say anything, didn't want to upset Mom any more than she already seemed to be. So Emily just prayed. She prayed and prayed and prayed. The car was silent, and Emily wondered if Kyle had actually fallen asleep. She wished she could fall asleep too. Maybe she would wake up and find out this had all been a bad dream. She also wished that she'd taken the time to use the restroom at McDonald's.

"I need a bathroom break," she finally said, interrupting the silence in the darkened car.

"I thought you went back at McDonald's."

"I can't help it if I have to go again," said Emily. "I think it was something in my cheeseburger."

Mom made a tired sigh. "Well, I suppose I could get gas in the next town. Can you wait that long?"

"I guess so."

"Or you can get out along the side of the road and —"

"No thanks," said Emily. "I can wait." Besides, she told herself, if Mom stopped at a gas station, there might be a pay phone she could use on her way to the bathroom.

But when they got to the next town, the bathrooms were off to the side and the pay phone was in obvious view of the car. There was no way Emily could use the phone without being seen by Mom. Unless…

"Don't you guys need to use the restroom too?" Emily asked when she returned to the car.

"You know, that's not a bad idea," said Mom. "It'll be at least three hours before we get to the motel. Kyle, maybe we should both use the facilities while we're here."

Then as they made their way to the restrooms, Emily made a fast break for the phone. But to her dismay, it was broken. The receiver was totally ripped off from the phone. "Why do people do things like this?" she said aloud as she walked back to the car.

"Hey, there's a pay phone in the office too," the gas guy called out to her.

"Thanks," she said. She considered running inside to use the phone, but felt too worried that Mom would be coming back and catch her and get mad. "I'm okay," she told him as she casually walked back to the car. What she really wanted to say was, "Help, I'm being held hostage by a crazy woman," but she knew that wasn't really true … or fair. She knew that most of all, Mom was just scared. And Emily also knew that Mom had good reason to be scared. If Dad did find them, he would take out most of his anger on Mom. And after that he'd take it out on Kyle. And, if he was mad enough, he might take the rest of it out on Emily.

The gas guy gave her a friendly nod and said, "Merry Christmas," before he went back inside to the dry office. He probably just assumed her family was off on a happy road trip, on their way to visit family for the holidays. If only that was the case.

Mom and Kyle returned and piled into the car. Soon they were back on the road again—a twisting, curving, dark, wet road that seemed to lead to nowhere, or worse. Emily kept imagining that they would meet their dad at the end of their travels. He'd be waiting for them in his big blue Ford Explorer. He'd make them all get out of the car, probably making arrangements to have it picked up and towed home, and then he would drive them back to Idaho. More than ever, Emily trusted Morgan's grandma's advice. They would be much better off back in Boscoe Bay!

"I still think this is totally crazy," Emily said to Mom.

"That's because you're a child." Mom's voice was getting more and more irritated sounding.

"I think it's crazy too," said Kyle.

"Well, lucky for you two, I'm the grown-up here, and I'm the one making the decisions for this family's welfare."

"But what about what Morgan's grandma said ..." Emily tried to remember exactly what she'd been told. "What would we do if Dad found us out on our own like this? We wouldn't have any friends or anyone to call for help. We don't even have a cell phone, Mom."

"That's right," said Kyle. "And if Dad ever does find us, you know he's going to be furious. Who knows what he might do?"

"That's exactly why we are making ourselves scarce. My plan is to become invisible."

"But how do you do that, Mom?" demanded Kyle.

"We'll go someplace where he won't find us. We'll change our names."

"But you said Dad wouldn't find us when we came to Boscoe Bay," persisted Kyle. "And you said by changing our names and living in such a small town, we would be safe."

"That's true," said Emily. "You did tell us that."

"Well, I'm sorry. I was wrong last time. But I won't be wrong this time. This time we won't just change our names, I'll change my social security number as well. I have a feeling that's what gave us away. And then we won't go for a small town this time. That was a mistake. We'll pick a large town. I think maybe somewhere in southern California ... somewhere warm."

"But we won't have the kind of community that we had in Boscoe Bay," said Emily, remembering Grandma's points now. "We won't have the kinds of friends and neighbors that can be a support system. In a big city, we'll just be lost in the crowd."

"Exactly," said Mom. "That's the plan — to be lost in the crowd."

Emily sighed. Maybe that sounded like a good plan to Mom, but it sounded lousy to Emily. She would do anything to get Mom to turn this car around and go back home to Harbor View Mobile-Home Park. It was ironic too, because Emily remembered how she'd felt when they first moved there last spring. She thought the place looked pretty crummy. But then she and her friends had fixed it up. They had their clubhouse. And now it seemed more like home than ever.

"Why don't you turn on the radio, Kyle?" Mom suggested. "It might help us to get our minds off of … other things."

But the drone of music didn't help Emily get her mind off of anything. All she could think was that they were making a big fat mistake. And the idea of Dad finding them out here with no one to stand up for them was truly frightening. Why couldn't Mom see that?

Emily leaned back into the seat, pulling the plush tiger-striped pillow toward her face. Morgan had helped her to sew this pillow, as well as several others for her bedroom. Then Emily remembered how they'd fixed up their clubhouse in the school bus, sewing pillows and curtains and all sorts of cool things. Tears filled Emily's eyes to think that she'd never get to go back to the clubhouse again. She would never go to another meeting, another party, or simply just a quiet escape to the bus. Worst of all, she would never see her friends again. Morgan, Carlie, Chelsea, and Amy were the best friends she'd ever had. And after a little more than six months, they were gone. It was so unfair.

She thought about the ski trip that she'd worked so hard to be able to go on, and how she'd actually gotten fairly good at snowboarding with Chelsea during Thanksgiving. And all for what?

Why are you doing this to me? she prayed silently. *God, I need you more than ever right now, and it feels like my whole life is just falling apart. Can't you do something? Can't you help me?* And, despite wanting to be brave like Anne Frank, the tears came pouring down. She pressed her face into the furry pillow to muffle the sound of her sobs. There seemed no point in upsetting Mom any more than she already was. Nothing was going to stop her from getting them far, far away. Life as Emily had known it was not only over and done with, it was out of control.

chapter six

Morgan hunkered down in the corner of Emily's darkened closet, curled into a tight little ball with her hands wrapped around her head as if that might somehow protect her from the evil force that was now prowling — make that stomping — through Emily's house. With what felt like a jackhammer pounding away in her chest, Morgan prayed desperately in silence. At least she hoped it was silent. Because what she really wanted to do right now was to yell and scream — and to cry out to God for help.

Morgan stared at the bright strip of light beneath the closed closet door. She wished she'd thought to turn off the overhead light in Emily's room. Hopefully that wouldn't lead the wild man directly to her hiding spot. But then she remembered that she'd left all the lights on throughout the house. Hopefully that would deter him for a while, long enough for Grandma to send help. And hopefully Grandma wouldn't come over here herself. She was under strict doctor's orders to remain at home, to remain calm. Suddenly Morgan was seriously worried about Grandma. And now she prayed for her. She prayed that Grandma would be sensible and not do anything to harm her health.

Then, for no explainable reason, she thought about what she'd read in that Anne Frank book just a few minutes ago. Somehow, it reminded her of how she felt right this very moment. Perhaps it was this hiding in a small space, the fear of being discovered. She felt helpless, almost less than human — like an animal being hunted. And, as silly as it seemed under her circumstances, she was more determined than ever that she would read that entire book — that is if she ever made it safely out of this closet. *Dear God, please help me,* she prayed urgently again. *Send help soon!*

"I know you're here!" His voice grew louder, as if he was closer now. Morgan guessed that he was in the hallway, probably going through the bedrooms. Maybe searching in the closets. Morgan curled even tighter into her ball, as if she might actually be able to vanish into the wall that was next to her.

"You might as well come out, Lisa! I've come for the kids, and I intend to take them with me tonight." Doors banged open and shut, and the crazy man kept yelling, stomping about, making threats, and using bad language. Morgan eased herself down onto her knees now as she tried to scoot more tightly into the corner, folding herself over into what was a praying position, which seemed entirely appropriate.

She felt something spongy with her hand. She gently squeezed it, trying to determine what it was. Then she realized it was one of Emily's flip-flops, a pair that Morgan had given her last spring. For a distraction from the monster who was still yelling and slamming things around, Morgan tried to recall what color the rubber flip-flops were. It seemed like they were baby blue. Almost the same color as Emily's eyes or the summer sky. Morgan tried to imagine that exact color and happier times as the sound of Emily's dad's footsteps and yelling came closer and closer. She knew he was in Emily's room now. And, clinging to the flip-flop, Morgan continued to pray in silence.

"Aha!" His voice softened a little now, as if he was trying to sound like a nice person. "I'll bet that you're the one who's home, Emily. Where are you hiding, Baby Doll? Where's Daddy's little girl?" Morgan thought his voice sounded about as genuine as a three-dollar bill, and she felt sorrier than ever for poor Emily. What a beast of a dad!

"I know you're here, Emily. I could hear you running through the house. Come out, come out, wherever you are."

Morgan's heart was pounding so hard now that she felt certain that half the neighborhood must be able to hear it. She flattened herself down even tighter against the floor and into the corner, wishing more than ever that she could simply disappear. But the footsteps were coming directly to the closet, and then the metal doors squeaked open.

"So there you are, Emily," said the man. His voice grew stern again. "Why didn't you answer when I called you? It's time to quit playing games, little girl. I'm taking you all back with me. Come on, now, Emily. Don't make me have to yank you by the —"

Without even knowing what hit her, Morgan stood up and turned to face this horrible man, looking him straight in the eyes. "I am not Emily."

He sort of blinked, and then got a mean-looking smile. "No, you certainly are not. You're the wrong color." He swore. "It just figures Lisa would bring my kids to a trashy neighborhood like this."

Morgan took in a deep breath and considered trying to bolt past this horrible man, although it looked hopeless. Perhaps this was a good time to let out a big, long scream.

"What are you doing in my wife's house anyway?" He stepped closer. "Did you break in to steal something, you little —"

"Put your hands in the air!" yelled someone from behind Emily's dad. "NOW!"

Emily's dad slowly raised his hands above his head. And Morgan slowly released the breath that she had been holding, the one she was going to use to scream for help.

"Now turn around, nice and slow." Morgan recognized the voice now. She peeked out to see Mr. Greeley with a metal baseball bat held high in the air like a weapon. The look on

Mr. Greeley's face was dead serious and a little bit frightening, although Morgan realized he was here to help her.

"Who the—"

"Never mind who I am," yelled Mr. Greeley. "Just keep your hands in the air before I knock your stinking head off. Morgan, girl, you get down low. Get yourself back in the corner of that closet, just in case I need to start swinging this thing."

Morgan did exactly as she was told. And this time she didn't feel quite as frightened.

"Who do you think you are?" demanded Emily's dad.

"I was about to ask you the same thing," growled Mr. Greeley.

Then Emily's dad spoke in a somewhat calmer tone. "Look, Mister. I have a legal right to be here. This is my wife's house. And I've come to take her and my kids back home with me. The law's on my side."

"We'll see about that," barked Mr. Greeley. "In the meantime, you keep your hands up high and you walk nice and slow into the living room."

"But you can't just come in here and—"

"And shut your trap!" yelled Mr. Greeley. "Before I start swinging this thing."

"But you—"

"Move it!" snapped Greeley.

Morgan listened as their feet slowly walked down the hallway and away. Emily's dad was still trying to reason with Mr.
Greeley, his voice seemed to be growing calmer and more
persuasive. Almost to the point where Morgan herself might
believe him — if she hadn't seen and heard what he was really
like. She just hoped that Mr. Greeley wouldn't fall for that
evil man's trickery. And she prayed that he'd keep that metal
bat handy until the police arrived, which seemed like it should
be happening any minute now. Morgan decided to count,
hoping that by the time she reached sixty, the police would
be here. But she had just said fourteen when she heard the
sounds of sirens approaching their neighborhood. And before
long she heard more voices and more footsteps. Still, Morgan
was afraid to move. What if the police had to use their guns?

"You can come on out now, Morgan," called Mr. Greeley's
voice.

Morgan slowly stood up, peering out of the closet to see
Mr. Greeley standing there. But the baseball bat was gone.
"Do the police have him now?" she asked warily.

Mr. Greeley nodded with a slight smile. "I hope I didn't
scare you too much with my tough-guy talk."

"No way, Mr. Greeley. You were my hero!" Then she
ran over and wrapped her arms around him in a tight hug.
And to her surprise he hugged her back.

"I'm just glad you're okay," he said as they both stepped
back.

Morgan's heart was still thudding like a marching band drum. She wasn't sure if it would ever stop pounding like that. "Thank you for rescuing me," she told him.

Mr. Greeley looked down at his feet. "Oh, it wasn't such a big deal. Just making sure you were safe."

"Morgan!" cried a frantic voice that sounded just like Mom.

"I'm in here," yelled Morgan, running straight for her Mom, grabbing onto her and holding tight.

"I was so worried!" cried Mom as she ran her hands over Morgan's hair then looked down and studied her face. "Are you really okay, Sweetie?"

"I'm fine, Mom. Everything's okay now."

"Grandma called me on my cell phone and told me what was happening. I was on my way home from work and driving as fast as I could, and then I got here and saw the police cars, and I was just so worried that —"

"Really, Mom," Morgan assured her. "I'm okay. Mr. Greeley came over here and saved me."

"Thank you so much, Mr. Greeley." Mom turned to him with tears in her eyes as she grasped his hand between both of hers. "I am so grateful that you were here. Thank you so much!"

He nodded shyly. "Just doing what needed to be done. That's all."

"But you should've seen him, Mom," said Morgan proudly. "He was just like some hero in a movie."

Mr. Greeley just waved his hand and said, "Nah, wasn't nothin' like that."

"Is that really Emily's dad in there?" asked Mom.

"I reckon so," said Mr. Greeley.

"It sure is," said Morgan with conviction. "I heard him talking and everything. He's a totally wicked man, Mom."

"The police said they'll be wanting to take our statements," Mr. Greeley told Morgan. "Are you up to talking to them now?"

"Sure am," said Morgan, standing straighter.

Morgan was relieved that Emily's dad had been removed from the house. Hopefully locked up for a long, long time.

"I'm Sergeant Moreno," said a policeman from the hallway. "I'd like to ask you some questions."

So the three of them sat on the couch while Sergeant Moreno began to ask Morgan and Mr. Greeley some basic things like their full names, addresses, and phone numbers. Morgan wished he'd hurry up to the important part. She was eager to tell her side of the story. But then he started with Mr. Greeley, asking what had made him come over to the Adams' house armed with a baseball bat.

"Well, I knew that Morgan was over here by herself," began Mr. Greeley. "But then I saw that strange car in the driveway. I knew that Lisa had run with the kids, and that she was in fear for her safety, saying that her ex-husband was dangerous. So I suspected it might be him over here, and I figured I might need a weapon with me. I didn't have time to call the cops."

"My grandma did," offered Morgan. "I called her when I thought something was up."

"That's right," said Mom. "My mother called me right after she called the police." Mom got a worried look. "In fact, if you'll excuse me, I'll give her a quick call to let her know all is well. She just had heart surgery."

Mr. Greeley answered a few more questions, and then Morgan got to tell the sergeant her side of the story, carefully giving him all the details.

"You have a good memory," Sergeant Moreno told Morgan. He turned to her mom. "Is your daughter always this descriptive?"

Mom smiled. "And you can trust her for giving it to you straight." She patted Morgan's hand. "I'm proud to say she is a very honest person."

"So, the intruder really said all those things?" the sergeant asked Morgan. "Made all those threats just like you said?"

Morgan nodded. "Except that I didn't use the swear words he used. I don't like to talk like that."

"Good for you."

"Mr. Adams is a very evil man," Morgan said finally.

The sergeant frowned. "Mr. Adams?"

"You know ... Emily's dad, the guy who broke in here."

"Oh ..." He jotted something down in his notebook.
"His name's not Adams. It's Chambers. Ken Chambers."

"That's right," said Mr. Greeley. "Lisa told me when they
first moved here that she had to use a new name to protect
herself and her family."

"So she and her children go by Adams now?"

"That's right," said Morgan.

"And where are they now?" asked the sergeant.

"We don't know for sure," said Morgan.

"Yes, we do," Mom said. "Or at least we know which way
they're heading. My mother just told me that Emily called our
house earlier. It must've been while Morgan was over here. It
seems that she and her family were in West Port at the time.
Emily called from a pay phone at the McDonald's there."

"So Grandma was right, they *were* going south," said
Morgan.

"They're probably still on the road," Mom told them.
"The plan, it seems, was to make it to the California border
and spend the night in a motel before they headed on in the
morning."

"I don't suppose you know the car's license number?"
asked Sergeant Moreno.

"I can describe the car," offered Morgan.

"You know, I think I've got the license number over there in my office," said Mr. Greeley quickly. "I didn't even think about that earlier."

"That's great," said the sergeant. "We can put out an APB, and hopefully get that family back here so that Mrs. Chambers can press charges."

"And we have a lawyer all set to help her," said Morgan.

"You do?" Mom gave her a surprised look.

"Yeah, a friend of Chelsea's dad wants to help her."

"You girls didn't waste any time, did you?" Mom winked at Morgan.

"We had to work fast," said Morgan. "Emily's part of our club. She's like a sister. We need to keep her here so we can stick together."

Sergeant Moreno smiled. "Well, you people are fortunate to live in a neighborhood where folks keep an eye out for each other. This whole thing could've turned out so much worse."

Morgan and Mom described Emily's family and the car to him now, right down to the dent in the right front fender.

"That's great," said the sergeant as they were leaving. He paused by the broken-down door. "But what about this?" He said to Mr. Greeley. "Should I send someone over to put a —"

"It's under control," Mr. Greeley told him. "Got a brand new door out in my shop right now. I'll have it back up even before the Adams — I mean the Chambers — get back here."

"Because they are coming back here," said Morgan. "Right?"

"Don't see why not," said the sergeant as he closed his notebook. Then he thanked them and they went their separate ways.

chapter seven

The car was quiet now. There was just the sound of the tires
hissing down the wet road, the thump-thump of the windshield wipers going back and forth, and the grainy hum of the
car's radio. Kyle had tuned to a popular coastal station, which
was slowly fading out as they continued driving south. Emily
was about to try talking some sense to Mom again when
she suddenly became aware of a different sound. Kind of a
whining sound, like a mosquito, but not on a wet rainy night
like this. She turned around in the backseat and peered back
behind them to see flashing blue lights slowly getting closer.

"Hey, Mom," she said quickly. "There's a cop car behind
us. With its lights on."

Kyle turned around in the front seat and looked back too.
"Yeah, Mom, it looks like they're chasing someone. You better
pull over and let them pass."

"I haven't seen anyone else on the road," said Mom as
she turned on her signal and slowed down and pulled over.

Emily continued watching the cop car and its flashing blue
lights. She expected it to zip right past them but, like them, it
too slowed down and stopped directly behind their car.

"What?!" said Mom with an alarmed voice.

"Were you speeding?" asked Kyle.

"No, I don't think so."

"You were driving a little fast," pointed out Emily.

"But not enough —"

"The policeman is coming to the car," said Kyle.

"I know," growled Mom. "You guys better have your seatbelts on."

"We do," said Emily.

"It's probably nothing," said Kyle. "Maybe you have a taillight out."

Mom rolled down her window. "Is something wrong?" she asked the policeman who leaned down with a flashlight, pointing it into the interior of the car and shining it all around as if he expected to find something illegal going on.

"Are you Lisa Chambers?" he asked.

"Well, I ... uh ... I am Lisa Adams," Mom stammered.

"May I please see your license and registration, ma'am?"

Mom fumbled to find her purse, searching for her wallet. "I don't understand," she was saying. "I wasn't speeding, was I?"

The policeman just waited until she finally handed him the items he wanted. Then he stepped away from their car and returned to his own car.

"He called you Lisa Chambers," said Kyle in a voice that sounded as scared as Emily was starting to feel.

"That means he's talked to Dad," said Emily. Her stomach got a hard knot in it.

"Do you think Dad's with him?" asked Kyle.

Emily turned around to peer into the police car, but thanks to the bright flashing lights she couldn't see if anyone else was inside.

"I don't know," said Mom.

"What are we going to do?" asked Emily, truly frightened now.

"I don't know …" Mom turned and looked back. "I could try to make a run for it."

"No," said Kyle. "That would be stupid."

Now Mom was starting to cry. "I *am* stupid," she said.

"No," said Emily in her firmest voice. "You're not stupid, Mom. Dad always tried to make you think that you were, but *you are not stupid*."

"Yeah, but leaving Boscoe Bay like this wasn't too smart," said Kyle.

"Kyle," said Emily in a warning voice. "That's not helping."

"He's coming back," said Kyle.

Mom rolled down her window again.

"Can you please step out of the car, ma'am?"

"But why?"

"I just need to talk to you," he said. "In private."

"Oh … okay." Mom turned and looked helplessly at Emily and Kyle.

"We'll be fine," said Emily.

Then Mom got out, and she and the policeman went behind the car to speak. Emily wished she could read lips. But it was obvious when he used the name Chambers, that the policeman knew something about their family.

"I know that's Dad behind this," said Kyle in an angry voice. "He's probably in that cop car right now, just waiting to haul us back to Idaho."

A cold chill ran through her. "What will we do?"

"I'm not going with him."

"But what if the law's on his side, Kyle? What if he forces us to go home with him?"

"I'm gonna make a run for it, Emily."

"No, Kyle, don't do that. That's crazy. We're out in the middle of nowhere."

"I'll just head due west," said Kyle. "Straight for the beach. I'll find a place to spend —"

"No, Kyle! You can't do that."

"I can't go back with him."

"But it's cold out there, Kyle. And wet. And the police would be looking for you."

"I don't care."

"Kyle, please," she pleaded. "It'd just make things worse if you did that … for you and everyone."

"Fine. You win. I'll stay." Then he swore.

"Kyle!"

"Sorry, Emily, but this just totally stinks. And I'll tell you what! I might go with Dad now, just cuz the cops are here. But I swear, the first chance I get, I'm gonna run for it. And I won't ever come back."

"Oh, Kyle!" Now Emily was crying again.

"Sorry, but I can't go back and live like that, Emily. Maybe it wasn't as bad for you. Dad always seemed to go a little easier on his Baby Doll."

"It was hard on me too, Kyle," sobbed Emily. "I don't want to go back either."

"Maybe you could run away with me."

"But how would we live? We're just kids, Kyle."

"Kids with parents who are totally nuts."

"At least one of them. You can't really blame Mom, Kyle. At least she was trying to get us away from him."

"Yeah, I guess she was right after all."

"Maybe so." Emily just shook her head.

"Dad's even got the law in Oregon in his back pocket. We don't have a chance against him."

"Yes, we do," said Emily suddenly.

"How's that?"

That's when Emily began to pray. Out loud this time. "Dear God," she prayed out loud, "Please, help us. We don't want to go back to live with Dad. He's a mean and wicked man. Please, please, help us out of this mess. I know you're my heavenly Father and that you love me more than any earthly father ever could. And I need you more than ever right now. We all do. Please, please, help us, dear God. Thank you. Amen."

"Like that's gonna change anything," said Kyle in a sarcastic tone.

"You don't know that."

"Yeah, right."

They sat silently in the car now. Emily turned around in the seat again, watching as the two figures stood in the drizzling rain, still talking.

"What can they possibly be saying for all this time?" demanded Emily impatiently.

"He's probably telling her that we have to go back with him." Kyle's voice was flat now, like he didn't care anymore, although Emily knew that he did. "The cop probably has some kind of court order from Dad. Maybe he's got a warrant for Mom's arrest. Dad probably accused her of kidnapping — that's a serious crime."

"Just like Mom said he would do." Emily kept watching. Now it seemed like Mom was the one asking the cop questions.

And it almost looked like she was getting mad as she shook a fist at him.

"You better look, Kyle," she said quickly to her brother.

He turned around in his seat to watch. "Wow, Mom looks ticked."

"I'll say." Emily felt even more worried. "I hope she doesn't smack that cop."

"That would not be good."

"Hang on, Mom. Don't do anything stupid," Emily pleaded.

Despite Mom venting at the cop, she did not strike him, and he remained calm. Then, after she quit raging, his expression grew almost compassionate, and he actually placed a hand on Mom's shoulder, nodding and saying something that Emily assumed was supposed to be reassuring.

"Maybe he's telling her that their jail cells are clean," said Kyle in a cynical tone. "Saying that the beds aren't too uncomfortable, and that prison food is pretty good."

"Yeah, sure," said Emily, joining his pathetic game. "And he's probably telling her that her children will be perfectly safe in the custody of their father, and that as long as she cooperates, she has nothing to worry about."

"I just thought of something." Kyle's voice got serious now. "If we thought it was bad being with Dad before, can you imagine how bad it'll be if she's locked up and we're stuck with him without her?"

Emily could not imagine. And she almost wanted to tell Kyle that she'd changed her mind just now, and that making a run for it might be their best bet after all. Sleeping on the beach in the rain might be tough, but not as tough as going back to Dad without Mom.

Even so, she had a feeling that running away would be a mistake in the end … and that it would backfire and they'd be in more trouble than ever. But she also had a strong feeling that this was the end of their little road trip. And suddenly she wasn't too sure she was ready for it to be over with now. She watched her mom's troubled face and felt guilty for the way she'd disagreed with Mom's escape plan right from the start. And she felt guilty for the way she'd slowed things down with phony bathroom breaks, which probably made it easier for the cops to find them. She also felt guilty for phoning her friends. For all Emily knew, that was how her dad had tracked them down. Emily felt worse than ever now.

If Mom went to jail, it would be partially due to Emily's interference. Perhaps Emily deserved getting stuck back with her dad. But her mom did not deserve getting stuck in jail. That was totally unfair!

chapter eight

"What a day you've had," said Mom as they walked away from Emily's house and back toward home.

"I'll say," said Morgan with a happy sigh. The rain had finally stopped and the Christmas lights on various houses in Harbor View made interesting reflections on the dark wet pavement. Morgan thought she'd like to paint something like this. It reminded her of a colorful beaded necklace against a piece of black velvet.

Mom ran her fingers through Morgan's curls as they crossed the street. "You still like your new hairdo?"

Morgan didn't answer. She didn't want to make Mom feel bad. She knew it had been expensive to have all her beaded braids removed a few weeks ago. But the truth was she really wished she'd never done it.

Mom paused on the porch. "You don't like it, do you?"

She looked up at Mom's bronze face, illuminated by the colorful Christmas lights on their house. Morgan kind of shrugged. "It's okay, I guess."

Mom started to smile. "Tell me the truth, Morgan."

"Okay, the truth is I did like the beaded braids better. I just didn't know it. I'm sorry, Mom. I know it was stupid to want to change my hair. I guess I thought it would make me more like my friends ... and then, after it was too late, I realized that I'd rather be more like me."

Mom threw back her head and laughed.

"That's funny?"

"No, Morgan, not funny like that. Just ironic, I suppose. Well, the truth is, I liked your beaded braids better too. In fact, I've been missing them."

"Me too," said Morgan as they went in the house.

"Well, if you want, you can get them back."

"Really?"

Mom nodded as she took off her coat and hung it on the hook by the door. "My treat, sweetie. I'll give Crystal a call this week."

Morgan hugged Mom. "Thank you! Thank you!"

"Hello there?" called Grandma from her recliner. "Is anyone going to fill me in on the rest of the story?"

"You go tell Grandma all the details of your latest adventure, and I'll start dinner," said Mom.

So, for the second time that night, Morgan retold the harrowing story of Mr. Chambers breaking into the house, her hiding in the closet, and Mr. Greeley's brave rescue.

"My goodness," said Grandma. "The good Lord was really watching out for you tonight, honey. I know I was praying my fool head off over here, stuck in this chair like this, but your mother gave me strict instructions not to set foot out of this house."

"And I'm glad you listened," called Mom from the kitchen.

"Well, I figured prayer was my best tool under the circumstances."

"Thanks for praying," said Morgan. "A lot of people have been praying today. And I can tell that it's made a difference. In fact, I should call my friends and tell them the good news. It looks like it's safe for Emily and her family to come back now."

Grandma nodded. "You go and call them, honey. I think I'll take a little nap before dinner. All this excitement has worn me out."

"Do you want me to help with dinner first?" Morgan asked Mom when she went into the kitchen.

"Call your friends," said Mom as she filled a pan with water. "Then you can help."

Morgan called Chelsea first, and for the third time tonight, she retold the story, slightly shortened this time.

"Wow," said Chelsea when she finished. "That's incredible."

"I know. It was a miracle."

"Well, I've sure been praying for one," said Chelsea. "I keep hoping that Emily will call me again."

"She called?"

"Yeah." Then Chelsea told Morgan about their quick conversation and how the lawyer was starting to research the case. "He really wants to help them."

"Well, he should call the police," said Morgan. "I'm sure they can fill him in a lot about Emily's dad and the charges against him already. Let me tell you, that guy is one scary dude."

"I'll let my dad know."

"Guess I better call the other girls. I know everyone has been seriously worried about Emily."

"Thanks, Morgan. Keep me posted."

"You too."

Next Morgan called Carlie, telling her an even shorter version of the still hard-to-believe story.

"No way!" shrieked Carlie.

"Way!" said Morgan, laughing.

"We wondered what was happening when we heard sirens in the mobile-home park. My dad went out to see, but since they were police cars, he wouldn't let us go out and look. I think he was afraid we'd get shot. I had no idea you were involved in that whole thing. I can't wait to tell my dad what was really coming down."

"Yeah, it was pretty weird."

"I'm sure glad I've been praying today."

"Yeah," said Morgan. "It's pretty much a miracle the way things are turning out. Anyway, I better call Amy now." So they said good-bye and Morgan tried Amy's house. When no one answered she tried the restaurant and got Amy on the second ring. She quickly retold the story once more. She was actually getting a tiny bit tired of it by now. Or maybe she was just tired in general.

"That's totally awesome," said Amy.

"Yeah," said Morgan. "I know …"

"So, does this mean we'll still have our Christmas party at the clubhouse on Thursday?"

"Sure, we have some really great reasons to celebrate now."

"And Emily gets to go on the ski trip too?"

"I don't see why not."

"*Cool.*"

"Yeah," said Morgan happily. "We are going to totally rock up there. I cannot wait!"

"Except for one thing," said Amy. "Uh, make that two."

"Huh?"

"Well, I ran into Jeff Sanders in town today."

"So?"

"So, he informed me that he and Enrico Valdez are both going on the ski trip."

"Why?" demanded Morgan. "They don't even go to our church."

"Well, neither do Carlie or I," Amy pointed out. "But I asked Jeff that exact same question, and it turns out that his uncle is your youth group leader, Cory What's-His-Name."

"No way. Cory is Jeff's uncle?"

"That's what he said."

"Well, that doesn't have to spoil anything for us," said Morgan with confidence. "Besides it's been a long time since those guys have bullied us, Amy. And they were actually pretty nice to us last summer. Remember the sand-castle contest?"

"And at least Derrick Smith won't be going," said Amy. "He's still in juvenile detention."

"So, we'll still have fun. A couple of boys can't ruin it for us."

"We'll have even more fun now that Emily is coming too. You know, Morgan, I was really praying hard for her today. I don't normally pray that much, but today I was asking God for a real miracle."

"It sounds like we all were, Amy. And it looks like that's just what we got."

"That is so cool — a real answer to prayer."

"Yeah. We have a lot to be thankful for." Morgan noticed Mom peeling potatoes. "But right now I need to go help make dinner."

"And I need to get back to work. It's starting to get busy here."

As Morgan hung up the phone, she decided it was time to ask God for something else. Emily and her family were still out there, still on the road and running for their lives. Morgan bowed her head and silently asked God to help the cops to find them, to turn them around, and to get them safely home. Then she went to help Mom in the kitchen.

"Do you think the cops will find the Adams — I mean the Chambers tonight?" asked Morgan as she peeled a potato.

"I hope so." Mom turned and adjusted the heat on the stove. "I know I wouldn't want to be in Lisa's shoes right now. She must feel so frightened ... so alone."

"Maybe we could make them something tonight," said Morgan suddenly. "Something to put in their house to help make them feel welcome and at home again."

"Oh, Morgan, that's a super idea."

"But what should it be?"

"Well, I know Lisa felt bad that she hadn't had time to make any Christmas cookies. And since Grandma's surgery, she hasn't been able to do much in the kitchen either. Maybe you and I could give it a try — as long as we keep it simple."

"I'm sure Grandma will have some good suggestions," said Morgan.

As it turned out, Grandma had lots of ideas. And, after dinner, the three of them — Grandma coaching from her recliner — managed to put together all sorts of wonderful things, including microwave fudge, caramel corn, Russian teacakes, and candy-cane cookies. Morgan even made a big Welcome Home sign on the computer while the cookies were baking. Then she found a spare string of colored lights that she thought would look pretty hanging up around Emily's new front door.

Finally, they put all their goodies together to make two yummy-looking platters that even impressed Grandma.

"I know it's not as good as what you would do," said Morgan as she held one out in front of Grandma.

"I think it's wonderful." Grandma smacked her lips after taking a bite of fudge. "I may have to retire from the kitchen altogether."

"Please, don't," begged Morgan. "No one is as good a cook as you are."

Grandma smiled. "Well, I'm looking forward to getting back to it after the New Year."

"It's getting late," said Mom, pointing to the clock on the wall.

"Wow," said Morgan. "It's almost nine."

"If we want the Chambers to have these tonight, we should take them over right away."

"We'll need to get the key from Mr. Greeley again," said Morgan.

"That's right," said Mom as she wrapped plastic wrap over one of the trays.

Morgan peered out the kitchen window and across the street to see that the lights on his house were still on in his house. "I think we're in luck too. Looks like he's still awake."

"We better hurry," said Mom.

"Hey, we should take him something too, Mom."

"You're right, Morgan." Mom opened the cupboard and reached for another platter and in no time they had it loaded up for Mr. Greeley.

Then they put on their coats and headed across the street where Morgan happily presented Mr. Greeley with the platter. "We made it ourselves," she told him. "Just a small token of our appreciation for saving my life tonight." She had rehearsed that little speech in her head as they walked across the street to his house.

He grinned and thanked them both.

"And if you don't mind, we'd like to leave these platters at the Chambers' house," said Mom.

"Sort of a welcome home," added Morgan, glancing across the street to see that the driveway was still empty. But at least the porch light was on. "Do you think they'll get home tonight?"

Mr. Greeley frowned. "I don't rightly know, but I sure hope they get home soon — safe and sound, of course." He handed Morgan the key.

"We'll bring it right back," she promised. Then she and Mom headed across the street to Emily's house. Mom put the goodies on the kitchen table, and Morgan taped her sign on the archway that led to the kitchen. Then, together, they hung the lights around the front door.

"Did you check to make sure they work?" asked Mom as Morgan stooped down to plug them in.

"Presto!" said Morgan as the colorful lights came on.

"Lovely," said Mom. "Now let's get this key back to Mr. Greeley."

"This should be a nice welcome for them," said Morgan as they stood in the yard and admired the string of lights.

"I feel just like one of Santa's elves," said Mom as they hurried across the street again.

"It's going to be hard to go to sleep tonight," said Morgan after they returned the key. She glanced back at Emily's house. "Knowing that they're still out there ... alone ... maybe still scared ..."

"Well, it should be a lot easier now that you know things are looking up for them," said Mom. "It's a much better scenario now than it was earlier today."

Morgan nodded. "Even so, I'm going to be praying extra hard until they get back."

"I think we all will be."

chapter nine

Just when Emily felt like she couldn't wait another second, Mom finally came back and got into the car. But then she just sat there in the driver's seat without speaking. She stared straight ahead as if she'd just spent the last ten minutes with aliens who had sucked every thought from her head.

"Mom?" said Emily. "What's going on?"

Mom said nothing.

"Come on," demanded Kyle. "We need to know what's up."

Mom slowly shook her head. "I'm not sure."

"Well, spill the beans, Mom," insisted Kyle. "What did the cop say to you?"

"Yeah," said Emily. "We're pretty much freaking here."

"The policeman told me that your dad was in Boscoe Bay."

"It figures," muttered Kyle.

"So he wasn't in the cop car?" asked Emily. At least that was something.

"No …" Mom shook her head again. "The policeman said he's in jail."

"In jail?" exclaimed Kyle and Emily at the same time.

"No way," said Kyle skeptically.

"That was my reaction too, but the policeman said that it was true."

"Why?" asked Emily.

"Apparently, he broke into our house."

"That loser," said Kyle.

"And apparently it was fortunate that we weren't there."

"I guess so …" said Emily, feeling slightly sick to her stomach now.

"But Morgan was there."

"Morgan?" Emily sat up straight in her seat. "Is she okay?"

"Yes, but apparently your dad threatened her."

"He threatened Morgan?" yelled Kyle. "I'd like to punch—"

"And then a man with a bat—"

"What?" demanded Kyle.

"The policeman said a neighbor, he said probably the manager—"

"Mr. Greeley!" yelled Emily.

"Yes," said Mom. "My guess too. Apparently Mr. Greeley showed up with a baseball bat and held your dad until the police arrived. Your dad's been charged with breaking and entering and, well, several other things too."

"That's fantastic," said Emily happily.

"Yeah," agreed Kyle. "I mean most kids wouldn't throw a party if their dad got arrested, but this is totally great."

"So the policeman wants us to turn around and drive back to Boscoe Bay now."

"Yeah!" said Emily.

"That's a five-hour drive," Mom pointed out. "We won't get back until midnight."

"That's okay," said Emily. "I don't mind staying up late."

"The policeman said we could stay in a motel if we were too tired to go back tonight," said Mom. "I don't know about you kids, but I feel exhausted."

"I can drive for you, Mom," offered Kyle. "I could use the practice, you know."

"So you kids really want to go back — back home — *tonight?*"

"Yeah!" they both cried at the same time.

Mom sighed and started the car. "I guess we can give it a try ... but no promises. It might be easier to just spend the night in the next motel and head for home in the morning."

"Whatever is best for you, Mom," said Emily. As badly as she wanted to be home tonight (right this minute in fact) she knew that Mom was probably as worn out emotionally as she was physically.

"Yeah," said Kyle. "You make the call, Mom. We won't complain."

"Well, let's get going and see how it goes."

"This is gonna be great, Mom," said Kyle hopefully. "We'll actually be *home* for Christmas."

"I hope so ..." Mom didn't sound completely convinced as she checked for traffic and then did a U-turn on the highway and started heading north. The police car did the same, following them — this time with the flashing blue lights turned off.

"And I need to tell you something else, Mom," said Emily. "I wasn't going to say anything until we stopped for the night and you could use a phone, but Chelsea's dad got you a lawyer. It's the guy I babysat for, Mr. Lawrence."

"And how did this happen?"

"Well, I guess Morgan told my friends about our situation. Chelsea called her dad and he set it up."

"See," said Kyle. "Morgan's grandma was right. It's better to take care of this kinda crud in a place where you've got friends to back you."

"I hope so," said Mom in a weary voice. "I really hope so …"

After a couple of hours, Mom actually did allow Kyle to drive. Emily wasn't so sure about this since Kyle had only been driving for a few months now. But because it meant they didn't have to stay in a motel, and that they'd be sleeping in their own beds tonight, she didn't protest. But she did pray. And eventually she fell asleep.

"Wake up," said Mom as she nudged Emily. "We're home."

Emily sat up in the backseat and blinked into the darkness. "Home?"

"Yes." Mom tugged her by the hand. "It's one in the morning, but at least you'll be in your own bed soon. We can unpack our stuff in the morning."

"Look," said Emily, pointing to the Christmas lights around their door. "Santa has been here."

"Yeah, right," said Kyle as he grabbed his backpack.

"Hopefully that doesn't mean that someone else moved in here while we were gone," said Mom.

"Isn't the rent paid up to the end of the month?" said Kyle.

"Yes — oh, dear!" said Mom. "I don't have a key. I gave it to Mr. Greeley."

"Chill, Mom," said Kyle. "I still have mine."

So he let them in. And they were barely in the house when Emily noticed the Welcome Home sign. "Look, you guys!" she cried. "Someone is happy that we're back." She suspected, by the bright colors, that this was Morgan's work.

"And look here," called Kyle from the kitchen. "Someone brought us goodies."

"A party!" exclaimed Emily.

"Well, I suppose a few cookies and some milk before bed might help us to sleep," said Mom as she opened the fridge.

Soon they were all seated around the little table, munching sleepily on the treats that Emily suspected had come from the Evans' house, although she knew that Grandma was still restricted from the kitchen.

"It is nice to be home," said Mom with a happy sigh.

"And nice to have such good neighbors," added Emily.

"And nice to have our lives back," proclaimed Kyle.

Emily wanted to ask about Dad. So many questions were racing through her head. She wondered what would happen next — and what would they do if they let him out of jail? And what if Dad decided to stick around Boscoe Bay? How could they stop him from making their lives miserable? Would he try to force them to go back with him?

Still, she was determined not to ask these questions. Not yet anyway. The good thing was that they were home again — and they had good friends nearby. Somehow God was going to help them sort this whole thing out. And Emily felt certain that she'd be sleeping well tonight.

It was so great to be back in her room — to be around her own things and to sleep in her own bed. And before she got into bed, she got down on her knees and thanked God for doing a miracle today. She asked him to work out the rest of the details for her family. And then she got into bed and let out a long tired sigh and fell quickly to sleep.

Emily woke up fairly late in the morning. Still, it felt good to be in her own room and her own bed and not some stupid motel down in California. She got up and walked through her house, smiling happily to herself. Sometimes you just didn't know how good you had it until it was almost gone. It was good to be home! She went into the kitchen and was surprised to learn from Kyle that Mom had actually gone in to work today.

"She said figured she might as well earn some money," he told her as he poured a bowl of cereal for himself. "She said we're gonna need it now."

"Was she worried at all?" asked Emily. "I mean about Dad being around?"

He nodded as he poured milk. "Yeah, I think so. She warned me to stick around the house all day. She said to keep an eye on you and to call her or the police if anything developed."

"Meaning if Dad came here?"

"Yeah …"

"It is kinda scary, isn't it?"

Kyle shrugged. "It's not that big a deal. We can always call Mr. Greeley or the cops. And I doubt that the old man will be outta jail this soon anyway. Oh, yeah, Mom said for you to call Chelsea about that lawyer dude. Then call Mom at work and give her the lowdown. She wants legal help as soon as she can get it. That was the main reason she didn't want to miss work today. She said the attorney's fees would probably really set us back a ways."

"Well, it'll be worth it," said Emily as she filled a bowl with cereal.

"And it'll be cool to have our lives back ... and with our own real names again. That Adams-family thing might've been funny at first, but it was getting kinda old."

"Yeah," said Emily. "Dad might be a jerk, but I like the name Emily Chambers better than Emily Adams."

After breakfast, Emily called Morgan. "We're back," she said, suppressing a giggle.

"I know," said Morgan. "I got up early this morning and saw your car in the driveway. You cannot believe what good self-control I've had not to run over and knock on your door and give you a big welcome-home hug."

"Well, what's stopping you now?"

"I'm on my way," yelled Morgan.

Soon Morgan was sitting at the kitchen table with Kyle and Emily, relaying all the details of the previous evening.

"Wow," said Kyle. "Were you pretty scared?"

Morgan nodded. "Oh, yeah ..."

"Good thing Mr. Greeley was on top of things," said Emily. "I can just imagine him with a baseball bat wielded like a club."

"Yeah, making his grim Greeley face," added Kyle. "I'll bet that put the fear of something into our dad."

"It did at first," said Morgan. "But then your dad tried to talk Mr. Greeley out of it."

"That sounds about right."

"Fortunately, Mr. Greeley held his ground."

"I need to call Chelsea," said Emily, eager to end the conversation. The more she heard about her dad, the angrier she felt toward him.

"Yes," agreed Morgan. "I called her to tell her you were home. We knew you must've gotten in late, so we all agreed not to bug you so you could sleep in."

"It was close to two in the morning," said Emily as she went for the phone and dialed Chelsea's number.

"I'm so glad you're home," squealed Chelsea.

Emily asked about the lawyer, and Chelsea said he was eager to speak to her mom.

"Does he want to call her at work?" asked Emily. "It's okay. Mom really wants to talk to him."

"Sure, I can have Dad let him know."

"Uh, I think my mom's a little worried about how much this will cost. I mean we're not exactly —"

"It's pro bono," said Chelsea.

"Huh?" asked Emily.

"Pro bono."

"What does that mean?"

"It means Mr. Lawrence wants to do it for free."

"No way!"

"Yep. He does stuff like that sometimes, especially around Christmas."

"Wow."

"Well, I better let my dad know that your mom's at work," said Chelsea.

"And I'll let my mom know that Mr. Lawrence will be calling her."

"Hey," said Chelsea, "we should have a meeting today. We need to plan our Christmas party."

"Good idea," said Emily. "I'll check with Morgan and get back to you, okay?"

"Sounds good."

Then Emily called the Boscoe Bay Resort, but Mom wasn't available. So she left a voice message saying that Mr. Lawrence would be calling her. "And by the way, Mom," she added. "He'll be doing it *pro bono*." Then she said good-bye.

"Pro what?" asked Morgan after Emily hung up.

"Pro bono," said Emily as if everyone should know what that meant.

"You mean like Bono the guy from U2?" asked Kyle. "He's a pro."

"U-who?" asked Emily.

"U2."

"This is starting to sound like a knock-knock joke," laughed Morgan. "Who is pro bono?"

"Not who," said Emily, "what."

"Okay," said Kyle. "What is pro bono?"

"Pro bono means the lawyer, Mr. Lawrence, wants to take Mom's case for free. Pro bono means free."

"No way!" said Kyle.

"Yep." Emily grinned. "It really is good to be back here with our friends, isn't it?"

"You bet it is," said Morgan.

"Hey, thanks for the goodies," said Kyle as he popped a piece of fudge into his mouth.

"Yeah," said Emily. "That was really nice of you."

"Comin' home was sweet," said Kyle with a wink. "But that made it even sweeter."

"Chelsea thinks we should have a meeting," said Emily. "To plan the Christmas party."

"You're supposed to stay home today, Em," Kyle reminded her.

"You mean I can't go with my friends to the clubhouse?"

He seemed to consider this. "Well, I suppose if they're all with you and they escort you back and forth."

"Like my own special security guards?"

"Yeah." He nodded. "I guess it's okay. And Chelsea has a cell phone, doesn't she?"

"So does Amy," pointed out Morgan.

Soon it was settled. The girls would have an official meeting at two.

"In the meantime," said Kyle, "you can help me put all our stuff away."

"You mean that giant heap by the front door?" asked Morgan.

"Yeah. I helped Mom unload the car before she went to work. It looks like it's gonna take all day to get everything put away." He shook his head. "I can't believe what we almost did."

Emily couldn't either. But the best part about it was that it seemed to be over. Still, it was disturbing to know that her dad was in town, and that he knew where they lived. But she tried not to think of that as they began to put things away.

chapter ten

With Morgan's help, Kyle and Emily got almost everything, including most of Mom's stuff, back into place by one o'clock. Then, as they were standing in Emily's bedroom, Morgan picked up the Anne Frank book from off her dresser.

"Are you done with this?" she asked Emily.

"Yeah. I read it in like two days."

"Can I borrow it?"

Emily tried not to look too surprised. "Sure, what makes you think you'd like it?"

"Like you said, Em, you can't judge a book by the cover." Then Morgan explained how she'd read a few pages and got hooked. "In fact, I was thinking about Anne Frank when I was hiding in your closet last night."

"Yeah, I can understand that. She was in hiding for years."

"Anyway, I can't wait to read it."

"Cool," said Emily. "And then we'll talk about it, like a mini book club."

"It's a deal." Morgan gave her a high five.

"Now, I'm starving," said Emily.

"Hey, why don't you guys come over to my house for lunch?" suggested Morgan. "We've got some really good leftovers that I can warm up for you. And I know Grandma will be happy to see you."

After a hearty lunch, Kyle entrusted Emily over to the friends who had gathered at Morgan's house. "I guess you're in good hands now," he said to her. "Just be careful and call me if you … well, you know …"

"And you be sure and lock the door at home," she quietly told him.

Then her friends escorted her to the clubhouse. They made jokes and pretended to be secret-service agents, but a small part of Emily knew that this was not completely a joke. It was still fairly serious business. But once they were locked inside the bus, Emily felt safer than ever.

"Man, is it good to be home!" she said happily.

"I brought treats," said Chelsea, opening up her backpack to produce some chips and soda. "Not the healthiest stuff, but I figured we had reason to celebrate."

For the next hour, the girls visited and laughed and enjoyed being back together again. Emily was relieved that they didn't spend too much time talking about her dad's unexpected appearance in Boscoe Bay. Her friends seemed to pretty much accept that he was a jerk and that it was in everyone's best interest that he was now in jail.

"I have an uncle who's in jail," admitted Carlie. "I didn't even know it, but when I told my dad about what happened with your dad, he told me about his older brother down in LA. I guess it was a similar situation. He'd been abusing his wife for years, and she finally pressed charges against him and he got locked up. My dad said it was a good thing."

Emily nodded. "Yeah, nobody should have to put up with that."

"Okay," said Amy, clapping her hands to get their attention. "We need to remember why we're having this meeting today." Then she reminded them that they were supposed to be planning for their much-anticipated Christmas party. The original idea, she pointed out, had been to dress up and invite family and friends from the mobile-home park and make it a really big deal.

"But what about this weather?" said Morgan, pointing out the window where the rain had just started to come down in buckets again. "Can you imagine everyone trekking out here to the bus and getting soaking wet in their nice party clothes?"

"You know, that party we had last summer was amazing," said Carlie. "But don't forget there were a lot of people here, and there was no way they could all be inside the bus at the same time."

"Yeah," said Morgan. "It was so warm that we had the party at the beach."

"Being outside of the bus on a rainy December night is not very appealing," said Chelsea.

"Not at all," said Amy. "And with everyone inside, it could get pretty crowded and stuffy."

"And I doubt the weather will cooperate," said Morgan. "This is, you know, the Oregon coast. Besides, do we really want everyone to know about our clubhouse?"

They briefly considered having their party in a different location, but that seemed to spoil everything. The point of the party was to be in the bus.

"I make a motion that we limit the party to just the five of us," said Amy finally.

"I second it," said Chelsea.

"And we can do our gift exchange," said Morgan.

"And we can decorate our Christmas tree," said Carlie with a sly grin.

"What Christmas tree?" asked Amy.

"I got a little one for the bus when I went out in the woods with my dad. I was saving it for the party."

So it was happily agreed — they would have their party on Thursday, just two days before Christmas.

"Hey, did you guys hear the news?" asked Amy. "About the ski trip?"

"You mean that Emily is going after all?" teased Carlie.

"No, I mean that our old enemies Jeff Sanders and Enrico Valdez are going."

"Why?" demanded Carlie.

So Amy explained, and Morgan tried to reassure everyone that it would be perfectly fine. "It's not like they'll be the only boys there," said Morgan. "And it's kind of cool that Jeff Sanders is Cory's nephew. I had no idea."

"And I think he's kind of cute," said Chelsea.

Emily wrinkled up her nose. "No way."

"Uh-huh," said Chelsea. "And he's nice too."

"Gross," said Emily, making an even worse face this time.

Chelsea poked Emily. "And I think you protest too much, Em. You know that Jeff likes you."

"Does not," said Emily. "Take it back."

"Chelsea's right," said Morgan. "Everyone knows that Jeff likes you, Emily. He's liked you ever since you moved here."

"Yeah, right, that day he and his bully friends knocked me off my bike. If that ain't love, I don't know what is."

They all laughed.

"You know," said Amy. "We really ought to be thankful for those boys."

"Why?" demanded Emily, still embarrassed by what Chelsea had just said about Jeff liking her. Okay, maybe he did like her, but Chelsea didn't have to go shooting her mouth off about it in front of everyone!

"Those stupid bullies were what originally got us girls together," proclaimed Amy. "It was their meanness that united us as friends."

"That's true," said Carlie. "And, to be fair, Enrico has been really nice to me this year. One day, right after school started, Andrea Benson bumped into me — on purpose I'm pretty sure — and I dropped my books all over the hallway floor, and Enrico stopped and helped me pick them up. I mean it was kinda embarrassing at first, having a boy helping me like that, and naturally Andrea made some totally lame comment, but it was kinda sweet too."

"Well, fortunately, Derrick Smith won't be on the ski trip," Amy informed them. "He's still locked up in juvie."

"You know, I feel sorry for him," admitted Emily. "He must be one pretty miserable kid."

"He sure likes making everyone else miserable too," said Carlie.

"You know what they say," said Morgan. "Misery loves company."

They laughed. But Emily couldn't help but feel sorry for poor Derrick. He was locked up and practically friendless. In a way, not unlike her own dad. Although she didn't feel sorry for her dad. She didn't care if he rotted in jail. And that thought alone made her want to think about something else.

"Well," said Emily. "I love being with you guys. And I am so totally jazzed to be home again. I've decided that it's true, you really don't know what you've got until someone tries to take it away."

"That's how we felt about you too," said Amy. "Suddenly you were gone, and it hadn't even been for a day and we really missed you."

Emily held up her soda can. "Here's to staying together!"

"To staying together," the others echoed.

chapter eleven

After Emily's friends escorted her home from their meeting, Chelsea asked if she could wait at Emily's house for her mom to pick her up.

"Sure," said Emily. "Unless you're afraid that my weirdo dad will show up and do something totally nutso." Emily tried to make this sound like a joke, but the truth was she felt a little uneasy. Just knowing her dad was in their town, that he had actually been in her house — even in Emily's own bedroom — was pretty upsetting. Creepy even. And, more than ever, Emily felt like she hated him. Not that it was a good feeling. It was not. But it was the truth.

"Nah," said Chelsea. "I'm not afraid. Besides my mom'll be here in a few minutes anyway."

"Any news?" Emily asked Kyle when they went inside.

He looked up from the video game he was playing. "Nope. All's quiet on the western front."

"Quiet is good," said Emily.

"Oh, by the way," said Chelsea. "My mom said to invite you guys to dinner tonight. She's going to call your mom at the resort to work it out. And the Lawrences are coming too."

"Cool," said Emily.

"My mom probably already gave your mom the details."

"Great."

"And while the grown-ups are talking, you and I can work on our wardrobe for the ski trip," said Chelsea. "It's not too soon to figure it out. The snowboarding pants I ordered arrived, and I can't wait for you to see them."

Emily nodded. "Sounds good." But what Emily was thinking was that she'd rather do that kind of planning with Morgan. Or at least include her. Still, she didn't think it would be proper to invite Morgan to Chelsea's tonight. And she didn't want to seem ungrateful to Chelsea for all the help her dad was getting for her family. Emily decided she'd just have to figure that out later. In the meantime, she felt certain that Morgan would understand.

"Chelsea, your mom's here," called Kyle from the living room.

"See ya tonight," said Chelsea as she grabbed her bag and left.

"So, I guess that means I have to go too," said Kyle after Chelsea was gone.

"You probably don't *have* to," said Emily. "But I don't see why you wouldn't want to. Besides, do you really want to be home alone ... you know, when dad is in town?"

He frowned.

"Besides, the Landers are pretty nice."

"Don't you mean pretty rich?" Kyle sighed as if giving in. "I guess I wouldn't mind checking out their crib. I've only seen that place from the driveway."

"They have a billiards room," said Emily. "And pinball machines and everything."

"Okay," said Kyle a little more cheerfully. "Works for me."

Emily returned to putting her room back together ... more carefully now. She checked out her closet for things she could take on the ski trip, but other than the Tommy Hilfiger outfit that Chelsea had given her, it was slim pickings. She had a feeling Chelsea would be in for a disappointment when it came to Emily's ability at any serious "wardrobe planning." Then Emily tried on the brightly colored polar fleece hat that Morgan had given to her as an early Christmas present. It was lively and cute, but she had a feeling Chelsea might not approve since it didn't have a designer label. But at the same time Emily was pretty sure that she didn't even care. Money, except when you really needed it for things like food or rent, was highly overrated.

When Mom got home, Emily was pleasantly surprised to see she was in a cheerful mood. She was actually humming a Christmas song as she hung up her coat. "Did you kids have a good day?"

"Yeah," said Emily. "Really good."

"And it was nice having the day off from work," said Kyle. "And luckily I still have my job at the station. The boss was pretty understanding. But he expects me to be there tomorrow for holiday traffic."

"We've been invited to dinner," announced Mom.

"We already know," said Emily. "Chelsea was here."

"So you'll be ready to go in about twenty minutes or so?"

"No problem," said Emily. She'd already changed into what she thought was an acceptable outfit of her best jeans and a sweater. Most of the times she'd been at Chelsea's had been pretty casual.

"And?" said Kyle impatiently. "Did you hear anything about Dad today, Mom?"

Mom smiled. "Yes. He's still in jail. Mr. Lawrence has already filed a restraining order on our behalf. It's looking really good."

Emily sighed in relief. "Aren't you glad we came back to Boscoe Bay?"

Mom nodded. "Yes. But I was in such a state yesterday, I just could not think straight. And, for the life of me, I could not imagine how this whole thing could possibly be resolved. But now I feel hopeful. After a brief conversation with the attorney, I think it might actually be achievable."

"And did you hear that he is doing the work ..." Emily tried to remember the terminology. "*Pro bono?*"

"Yes, I could hardly believe it."

"We're gonna get through this," said Kyle.

"Absolutely," said Mom. "Now let's get ready to go. Kyle, can you put on a clean pair of pants?"

Kyle may have had on clean pants, and Emily had even worn a designer sweater that Chelsea had given her, and Mom looked nice, still wearing a dark pantsuit from work, but just the same, Emily felt like their family was out of place as they sat around the Landers' dinner table. She tried not to think about it too hard, and she hoped her mother didn't notice anything, but she felt uncomfortable.

It was weird, because she'd eaten at Chelsea's house lots of times, but it had never been like this. Tonight felt formal. Dinner was "served" in the fancy dining room with fancy dishes and crystal and silver and candles. Mr. Landers and Mr. Lawrence — both still dressed from work — had on business suits, Mrs. Landers had on a pretty red pantsuit, and even Chelsea was dressed a bit more nicely than she had been earlier today.

Not that this was just about the clothes … although Emily knew that her family looked shabby and poor next to these wealthy people. But it felt as if something more was happening here. The more the grown-ups talked about her family's troubles and how Mr. Lawrence would be helping them, the more Emily felt like her family did not belong here — not socially anyway — and the more she felt like her family was really just a charity case. A Christmas project to make the others feel good. And Emily hated feeling that way. It was so ungrateful … and judgmental.

"Can we be excused?" asked Chelsea after dessert was mostly finished. "We need to make some plans for our upcoming ski trip."

"You mean wardrobe plans," teased her mom.

"Of course," said Mr. Landers. "I'm sure this conversation must be boring to you kids."

Emily tried not to sigh in relief. She considered asking Kyle to join them, but she wasn't sure if Chelsea would be okay with that. Fortunately, Mr. Landers offered Kyle the use of the game room, and her brother seemed happy to make an escape too.

Once safely in Chelsea's room, Emily flopped into a chair. "Whew," she said. "Glad that's over."

"I know," said Chelsea. "Grown-ups can go on and on about the most boring details." She opened up her closet and started tossing out items of winter clothing. "I thought you could borrow some stuff for the ski trip," she said. "You know, like you did for the Thanksgiving trip."

"Oh, that's okay."

"Huh?" Chelsea turned and looked at her. "What do you mean?"

"I mean, that's okay. I don't need to borrow anything."

"Don't you wanna look hot up there?"

Emily shrugged. "I don't know …"

"Are you feeling okay?" Chelsea came over and actually put her hand on Emily's forehead as if to see if she was running a temperature.

Emily forced a laugh and pushed her hand away. "I'm not sick."

"But something's wrong." Chelsea studied her face closely. "What?"

"I think I'm just kinda tired and overwhelmed from everything." Emily knew that was partially true, but she also knew that wasn't the total problem just now. Still, she wasn't sure she wanted to say what it was that was bugging her. Maybe it was really just her imagination.

"I'm sorry," said Chelsea. "I guess I'm not being very understanding. I just figured there wasn't much time, and we should plan what we're going to wear—"

"You know what I'd like to do?" said Emily, sitting up suddenly.

"What?"

"I'd like to plan what we're going to wear with all the girls in the club."

"Hey, that's a great idea."

"Yeah. Because most of us don't really have ski clothes. I mean who needs them unless you go up there a lot. So maybe we could sort of pool our things together and share stuff and have a packing party or something."

"That sounds like fun." Chelsea tossed her clothes back into her closet, not even bothering to hang them up. Of course, they had a housekeeper who took care of that.

"Maybe right after Christmas," suggested Emily.

"We can have it here if you think that's okay." Now Chelsea frowned. "I know, I probably come on too strong sometimes. But you know how I am about fashion."

Emily smiled. "Yeah, you really get into it."

"You got that right." She grabbed a magazine. "Hey, look at this pair of jeans. They are so cool."

So Emily humored Chelsea for a while, poring over her latest fashion rags and acting interested, until she finally she got so bored that she asked if they could go play a game of pool with Kyle.

"Okay," said Chelsea as she tossed a magazine aside. "That actually sounds like fun."

"I'm sure Kyle will appreciate some company ... even if it is just us."

"You know, Kyle is getting to be really good-looking."

Emily rolled her eyes at her. "Puh-leeze."

Chelsea laughed. "Well, he is, Em. His skin is all cleared up now, and he got taller, and I can't help it if I noticed that he's looking really —"

"Fine, fine," said Emily quickly. "You think my brother is a hottee. Now let's not talk about it anymore. Eeuw."

But as they went downstairs, Emily wondered if Chelsea wasn't just starting to get a little too boy crazy. That was the second time today that she'd gone on about boys.

"Hey, Kyle," said Chelsea as they went into the game room. "We chicks wanna challenge you to a game of pool. You in?"

"You're on," said Kyle, picking up a cue.

Chelsea put some songs into the jukebox, and Emily helped Kyle to get the balls set up. She wondered if Kyle would be surprised to see that her pool skills had improved a bit since hanging with Chelsea. They'd played quite a few games down here in the past several weeks.

But the more the three of them played, the more irritated Emily felt at Chelsea. It was like she was actually flirting with Kyle. And it made Emily feel very uncomfortable. For one thing, Chelsea was only thirteen — three years younger than Kyle! For another thing, Kyle seemed to be enjoying the extra attention. But in Emily's opinion, Chelsea was acting like a total idiot. Emily was getting downright disgusted with both of them. Thankfully, Mom broke things up.

"Hey, kids," she called from the top of the stairs. "I hate to spoil the party, but it's been a long day for me, and I have to work tomorrow."

"That's okay," said Emily, perhaps a little too eagerly, as she put away her pool cue.

"Let me put this last one away," said Kyle, pocketing the eight ball in the corner pocket.

"You are such a good shot," said Chelsea.

Kyle grinned. "Thanks. And thanks for the games."

"Well, thanks for cleaning our clocks," said Chelsea, gently punching him in the arm.

"Anytime," said Kyle.

It was all Emily could do not to roll her eyes and groan. "Thanks for everything, Chelsea," she said instead. "See ya."

chapter twelve

The next day, Emily couldn't wait to get to Morgan's house. The plan was to work on the Christmas presents they'd been making for the other girls. And it felt so good to hang with Morgan and just be a regular kid again, creating things that would be fun to give to her friends. Whether it was beading or knitting or sewing, Emily just focused her attention on each project and enjoyed hanging with Morgan.

"This is so great," Emily said as they took a break to make themselves and Grandma some lunch. "I can't believe I almost lost all this."

"Me neither," said Morgan as she poured the second can of chicken and rice soup into the pan. "So, how's it going … I mean with your dad and everything?"

Emily could tell that Morgan was still a little uncomfortable with all this. For that matter, so was Emily. Still, she'd been fairly honest with Morgan. She'd told her that — although she was relieved that her dad was locked up — it was still hard knowing that he was in town. She hadn't told Morgan that she hated him. As a Christian, Emily knew she wasn't supposed to hate anyone. Even her enemies. She also knew that there was a commandment that said kids were supposed to respect their parents. This one really confused her. How was she supposed to respect someone like Dad?

"My mom is feeling pretty hopeful that the lawyer is going to get it all straightened out before long."

"No chance of your dad getting out of jail?"

"Not according to the lawyer. He said that bail is set pretty high, and it doesn't look like anyone is jumping in to help him out. Sounds like he'll be in there a while."

"How do you feel about that?" Morgan's forehead creased as she stirred the soup. "I mean, I realize he is your dad. Does it bother you knowing he's locked up?"

"It would bother me more if he wasn't." Emily laid a slice of cheddar cheese on top of a piece of bread.

Morgan nodded. "Me too."

"But the lawyer has already got a restraining order made out."

"That's good."

"So, even if he did get out, he would be in serious trouble if he came near any of us."

"You guys should probably get cell phones," said Morgan.

"Yeah ... Mom's thinking the same thing."

"I wish my mom was thinking that too." Morgan laughed. "I keep hinting that a cell phone would be a good Christmas present. But so far, I don't think she's buying it."

"Well, if we do get cell phones, my mom made it perfectly clear they will be those cheap ones, the kind that are only for emergency use."

"At least we have friends that have them." Morgan put one of the cheese sandwiches onto the hot grill, and they both watched it sizzling.

"Speaking of rich friends …" began Emily. "My mom and Kyle and I had dinner at the Landers, last night." She sliced another piece of cheese and handed it to Morgan, who was now putting the sandwiches together.

"Really?"

"Yeah. Mainly so that Mom could meet the lawyer and they could talk and stuff. But it was this really formal dinner with lots of silverware and glasses, and I felt like a fish outta water. I think Kyle did too. Of course, he didn't admit it."

Morgan laughed as she set the next sandwich on the grill. "Yeah, I just do not get why some people want to make something as simple as eating food so complicated."

Then, without even thinking, Emily began making fun of the Landers and all their fancy forks and things, but then she felt bad. After all, Chelsea's family was really helping hers.

"Sorry," said Emily. "I don't think that was very nice."

Morgan nodded. "I understand."

"I don't want to seem ungrateful … I just don't really want to feel like I owe them something too. You know?"

"You don't owe them a thing, Emily." Morgan pushed her glasses back up her nose and then shook her finger at her. "You shouldn't think that way. Just because one person helps another person doesn't mean that anyone owes anyone anything. Not if you're doing it for the right reasons anyway." She turned and gave the soup a stir.

"I'd like to believe that," said Emily.

"Well, then you better."

Then Emily told Morgan about the packing party that Chelsea wanted to have at her house before the ski trip.

"Why?" said Morgan as she flipped one of the grilled-cheese sandwiches.

"Well, I guess it was kinda my fault," admitted Emily. "Chelsea was trying to share some of her ski clothes and stuff with me — because she wants me to look all cool and fashionable when we go on the ski trip — and it sort of hurt my feelings, although I didn't let her know. And now that I think about it, I was probably pretty ungrateful about that too. I mean I shouldn't have been offended by her generosity."

"Oh, I don't know …"

"Anyway, I suggested that we could all get together, you know, since most of us don't have ski clothes or much snow stuff. I thought we could all share and plan our outfits together."

"Oh, I get it," said Morgan. "I guess that's a nice idea. And Carlie and Amy will probably appreciate it too."

"Poor Amy," said Emily. "She's so much smaller than the rest of us, she probably won't find anything she can use."

"Hats and scarves," said Morgan. "And I actually have several of those."

"Well, I guess it might be fun."

"You bet it'll be fun," said Morgan.

"Maybe we should do it at the clubhouse instead of Chelsea's," suggested Emily. "That way it might not feel as much about money and things as just having a good time."

"That's a great idea!"

So, after lunch, they called their friends and arranged to have everyone meet at the bus on the day after Christmas. Chelsea wasn't sure it was such a good idea, but Emily finally convinced her it would be fun, saying they could do fashion walks down the middle aisle of the bus, and pretend that they were on a fashion shoot.

"Hey, I'll bring my digital camera," said Chelsea, now fully on board.

"And don't forget that Amy is tiny," said Emily. "If you have any old things, you know, ski stuff that you've outgrown, bring them for her."

Then Emily and Morgan spent the rest of the day working on Christmas presents, listening to music, and just hanging. In fact, that's how Emily spent the next two days.

Then on Thursday, the girls got together at the clubhouse for their Christmas party and gift exchange. Morgan and Emily got there early, putting on some Christmas music and turning on the strings of lights. Then they set out the Christmas cookies that they'd made and frosted just yesterday. Then the others arrived, and Carlie set up the little Christmas tree in the driver's seat, and they decorated it with ornaments from home.

After that, they took turns opening their Christmas presents, starting with the ones from Morgan. She'd made each of the girls a brightly colored pair of polar fleece socks and matching hats.

"You might want these for the ski trip," she told them as they tried them on. Then Emily gave her friends the hand-made beaded chokers that Morgan had helped her to make. Each one came with its own little drawstring bag, which Emily had sewn on Morgan's sewing machine. She had specially designed each necklace with each friend in mind. Everyone seemed to really like them, which made Emily feel good.

Carlie gave them all hand-painted ceramic dishes, which she explained she had decorated herself at the local pottery shop, personalizing each one with the girls' names before they were fired in the kiln. "You can use these to put your jewelry and things in," she told them happily.

After that, Amy gave them each a "free lunch" gift certificate for her family's restaurant, along with a bag of fortune cookies. "Okay, I guess I'm not as clever as you guys, because I didn't exactly make these myself," she admitted. "But it was the best I could do under the circumstances. We have been busier than ever this past week." She glanced at her watch. "In fact, don't let me forget that I have to get back there by four."

"Well, I didn't make my gifts either," said Chelsea as she handed them each a small rectangular box wrapped in metallic pink paper and tied with a matching ribbon. Chelsea had insisted on going last, and Emily had a feeling it was because her gifts would be the most impressive — or at least the most expensive. "I didn't know we were supposed to."

"Well, it wasn't exactly a rule," said Morgan. "But it was suggested. We didn't want anyone to feel pressured to go out and buy things."

"Especially after we all worked so hard to pay our way for the ski trip," Carlie pointed out as they opened Chelsea's packages. Beneath the shiny pink paper was a long, narrow, black velvet box with a fancy gold B in one corner.

"Ooh," said Amy with excitement, "This looks like it's from Bernstein's. My dad gave my mom a diamond necklace that was in a box like this."

"Well, don't worry," said Chelsea. "No diamonds are involved."

The girls all laughed, but no one had opened a box yet.

"Come on," Chelsea said eagerly. "Go ahead and see what's inside."

Emily ran her finger over the plush velvet box. She knew that Bernstein's was the jewelry store downtown. She'd never been in the shop, but she could tell by the window displays that it was a pretty nice store — and expensive. The other girls were beginning to ooh and aw, so Emily knew she needed to open her box too. And when she did, she saw that it contained what looked like a nice charm bracelet.

"See the little school bus," gushed Chelsea. "Isn't it just too cute?"

"It's like our bus," said Carlie.

"These are beautiful," said Amy as she held her bracelet up to the light. "They must've been expensive."

"Not as much as gold ones would've been," said Chelsea. "Mom nixed that idea right off the bat. But these are sterling silver." She held out her own wrist now. "See, I have a bracelet too. Obviously, the school bus represents our clubhouse, and the initial is for your first name, so we don't get them mixed up."

"What about you and me?" said Carlie. "We're both C's."

"Yeah, I figured that could be a problem, so I got an L put on mine, for my last name. And see the little snowboard. That's for our upcoming ski trip."

"Cool," said Amy.

"Yeah, thanks," said Morgan. "These are really nice."

They all thanked her, and everyone seemed happy. And yet Emily was curious. She wondered if Chelsea's bracelets were meant to replace their old beaded ones that she and Morgan had made last summer. Still, she decided not to bring this up. She didn't want to seem ungrateful or to stir up any problems at their Christmas party. Besides, what was the harm in wearing two bracelets? Because Emily knew that she had no intention of giving up her old one. It meant too much to her.

Next they had refreshments. And as they munched, they joked and chatted and enjoyed their own little party of five. In the background, cheerful Christmas music played, and for a moment, Emily just sat there looking at her four good friends. She still couldn't believe how close she had come to losing all this. As a result, she thought of her dad, but these were not happy thoughts. In fact, every time he came to mind, her stomach would tie itself into a tight knot, and she would begin to feel a combination of anger and fear. More and more, she felt that she hated him. And sometimes she wished he were dead.

"What's wrong, Em?" asked Morgan.

"Yeah," said Carlie. "You look kinda bummed. Is everything okay?"

"Sorry." Emily shrugged. "I guess I was just remembering stuff … you know … about how my family almost left Boscoe Bay for good and everything."

"Well, don't think about that," said Amy. "You're here. You're with us. And everything is cool."

"That's right," said Chelsea. "Celebrate!"

And so Emily pasted a big smile on her face and pretended to be totally happy. But underneath it all, she was not. Underneath it all, she was just plain mad — she was angry at her dad and for how his presence in her town and in her life was nothing but a great big pain. And it felt like her anger was starting to eat away at her.

chapter thirteen

Emily could hardly believe that it was the day before Christmas. So much had happened this past week, it had felt as if the time had flown by. And now it was December 24th, and Emily planned to spend a quiet day at home. Mom and Kyle both had to work during the day, and Morgan was next door helping her mom and grandma get things together for their Christmas. She had invited Emily to join them, but since Emily had been practically living over there the past few days, she decided to give them a break today. Plus, her family would be going over to celebrate Christmas with them tomorrow anyway.

For today, Emily's plan was to wrap Kyle's and Mom's Christmas presents and then straighten up the house. But she'd finished that a lot quicker than she'd expected. Her presents were already tucked beneath their tree, and their house was all tidy and neat. She walked around a bit, just taking a moment to enjoy the results of her efforts. Their place was really pretty cozy now. So much better than when they'd first come here last spring. In fact, that seemed like a long time ago now.

She remembered how lost she'd felt when they moved into this house. It was so much smaller and shabbier than the house they'd left behind. But even so, Emily had been relieved to get away from her angry father. It had been worth the sacrifice. Now — if only he hadn't tracked them down — life might be nearly perfect. She'd been trying not to dwell on the fact that her dad was still in town. It was too disturbing. But at least, according to their lawyer anyway, he was still in jail. Although the rumor was that he was trying to borrow bail money from his family in Idaho. Probably from Aunt Becky. She was still pretty clueless when it came to the true character of her "baby brother." She had always tried to protect him, always acted as if he was blameless.

Despite her resolve not to, Emily thought about her dad. She sat down beneath the Christmas tree and wondered what it felt like to be locked up in jail. What would if be like to be restricted to a small space like that? She remembered the book she'd just read, and how Anne Frank and her family lived in an attic space for several years. In a way, that must've felt like prison too. And yet they had done nothing wrong.

Then Emily wondered how it would feel to be in jail during Christmas. How would it feel to think about other families enjoying each other, enjoying all the fun parts of Christmas? She felt an unexpected jab of pity just then — sort of how she felt when she thought about Derrick Smith being stuck in juvenile detention. Not that both those bullies didn't deserve to be locked up. They did. But the image of her dad sitting alone behind bars made her feel sad. Okay, it was sad mixed with mad. And she definitely didn't want him to get out. In fact, it worried her a lot to think that someone like Aunt Becky might possibly post his bail.

If only things could be different — if only her dad could be different — but that didn't seem possible. As it was, she hoped he'd be stuck in jail for a long, long time. She hoped he'd never get out. When she considered how much he'd hurt her family … how he'd frightened and threatened her very best friend. Well, Emily really didn't feel too sorry for that man. Not really.

Still, she knew enough about the Bible and Jesus' teachings by now to know that Christians were supposed to follow Jesus' example and to forgive those who hurt them. She also knew they were supposed to pray for people who were enemies or wanted to hurt them. The truth was she had never really done it much before. She'd never really had the need to do it. Until now. And yet she wondered how she could forgive a man who had brought so much pain into her life? How was that even possible?

Emily stretched out on the matted-down carpet beneath their Christmas tree. She put her hands behind her head and closed her eyes as she pondered these troubling questions. It felt wrong to *not* forgive … and yet how was it possible to forgive someone you still felt mad at, someone who had hurt you badly, and someone you sometimes hated? She went round and round with these questions until she finally knew it was useless — there really was no good answer. Just more questions.

That's when she did what her pastor often recommended. She took the whole thing to God. She asked him to show her what she needed to do about this perplexing problem. She asked God to guide her. And, just like that, the answer came to her. And it seemed simple enough. But simple didn't always come easily.

First of all, she knew she needed to forgive her dad, and second of all, she knew she needed to pray for him. The problem was she didn't know how to do that. It seemed impossible. So, right then and there, she asked God to help her. And, right then and there, although she didn't really feel like it, she decided it was time to forgive her dad.

So she told God she could only do this thing with his help, and she asked him to help her. Then help seemed to come, and she actually did forgive her dad. She even said the words out loud. More than that, she actually prayed for her dad. She asked God to reach out to him, to help him see what he was doing wrong. "And help him," she prayed, "to see that he needs you, dear God. Show my dad that he can't change and live a good life without your help. And tell him that you love him. Thank you. Amen."

When Emily opened her eyes and looked up at the Christmas tree, she realized the colored lights were all blurry and fuzzy now ... because she was crying. And that's when she knew that it was for real. She knew that God really had helped her to make this step to forgive her dad. She also realized that it felt as if a heavy weight had been lifted from her — and that for the first time in a long time she felt truly happy.

She felt so happy that she even put on some music — a lively Christmas CD that Morgan had given to her just yesterday. And Emily cranked it up and did a little happy dance around the Christmas tree. And as she danced, she thanked God for helping her. And she thanked him for sending his only Son to share forgiveness with everyone — even her dad!

Then when she was too tired to keep dancing, she collapsed onto a chair. And that's when she got the strongest urge to write her dad a letter. She still had some Christmas cards leftover from the ones she'd given to her friends and few special teachers at school. She took one out and wrote his name on the inside of the card. Then she took out a clean piece of paper and wrote a heartfelt note to her dad.

Dear Dad,

You're probably surprised to get this card from me, but I was thinking about you today. And because I'm a Christian now, I know that God wants me to forgive you for all the times you hurt Mom and Kyle and me. So I just prayed a little while ago, and God helped me to forgive you. I'm also going to be praying for you now because the Bible says to pray for your enemies. I don't like to think that my dad is my enemy, but you've done some pretty mean things to us ... the kinds of things that enemies do to people they don't like. So, anyway, I will be praying for you.

I don't know how long you'll be in jail, and for your sake, I hope it's not too long. But I hope it's long enough for you to think about all the things you've done and the way you've hurt us. I hope you stay there long enough to feel sorry for your mistakes. And then I hope you'll go back to Idaho and leave us alone. I heard enough of what Mom's lawyer said to know that the law is on our side now. We've been in Oregon for more than six months, so that means you can't force us to leave. You probably know this too. Anyway, I hope that someday Kyle and I will be able to talk to you. Someday when you don't want to hurt us anymore. And I hope that your life gets better, Dad. I hope that you get some help with your anger problem. And I hope that this Christmas, even though it's probably hard, is like a turning point for you. I'm praying that you will ask God for help and that you'll give your heart to him. I know he's helped me through some pretty tough times.

From Emily

Emily looked at the ending of her note. *From Emily* sounded a little formal and sort of mean. So she crossed out "From" and replaced it with "Love." She figured that would make God happy since Christians were supposed to love others, whether others deserved it or not. Then she put the note inside the Christmas card, wrote Dad's name on the front, put on her coat, and walked to town. It was actually a pretty nice day. No rain, no wind. Of course, there was no snow either. That was probably the only thing she missed from her old home in Idaho. But she would rather be here without snow than in Idaho with three feet of it. Besides, she would have plenty of snow in a couple of days.

It was fun walking through town. Christmas music was being played outside, and the town's Christmas tree was lit up, as well as colorful lights in most of the shops. People were busily hurrying around, probably doing their last-minute tasks before Christmas. Emily smiled at people and said hello to ones she knew. She even paused and put some change into the Salvation Army pot. Then she walked on to City Hall. She wasn't absolutely certain that her dad was in the jail there, but she figured there was a good chance that he was.

Then, as soon as she went through the entrance, she felt self-conscious. She wondered if she was making a big mistake in coming here. And what if Mom got mad at her for doing this? Still, Emily knew in her heart that it was the right thing to do. And so she went up to the front desk.

"Can I help you?" asked a policewoman.

"Uh, I have something to be delivered," said Emily. She set the envelope on the desk. "It's for my dad."

The woman smiled. "Oh, is he a policeman?"

"Uh, no …" Emily took in a quick breath. "I think he's in jail here."

The woman nodded. "Oh …"

"Do you think someone could give him this Christmas card for me?"

"It will have to be opened and inspected first," the woman told her. "Are you okay with that?"

Emily shrugged. "Yeah, I guess so."

"It's not that we don't trust you. It's just a policy. Some people try to sneak things in here — things that aren't allowed."

"Oh, well, there's nothing like that in there."

The policewoman smiled. "No, I didn't think so. And I'm sure your dad will appreciate that you thought of him."

"I thought he might be feeling a little sad, you know, being in here for Christmas. I mean I think he *needs* to be here and everything. Still, it's probably hard on him."

"Well, if it makes you feel any better, I've heard that the Christmas dinner served here is pretty tasty."

Emily smiled. "That's good."

"You have a Merry Christmas now."

"You too." Then Emily turned and walked out. Sure, it hadn't been the easiest thing in the world to do, but she was so glad she'd done it. And she knew she had only been able to do it with God's help. She also knew this was going to be a really great Christmas.

faiThGirLz!
the beauty of believing

PROJECT: *Ski Trip*

CHECK OUT
this excerpt from book
seven in the Girls of 622
Harbor View series

Melody Carlson

"This has been the best Christmas of my entire life!" Carlie said happily as she helped her mom clean the kitchen. It was the day after Christmas, and according to Mom, their house was "a big fat mess." Carlie didn't think it looked that bad. Still, she hadn't complained about helping this morning. Mostly she just wanted to get these boring chores finished so she could get to the clubhouse in time for this afternoon's meeting.

Her mother stopped scrubbing the countertop and peered curiously at her now. "What made this Christmas so special for you, Carlotta?"

Carlie paused from sweeping as she considered an answer to Mom's question. The truth was Carlie wasn't *only* thinking of Christmas with her family, although it had been nice enough. But she was thinking about her friends too. She was thinking of the fun she'd had with them, and better yet, the fun that was just around the corner. But if she said that, it might hurt Mom's feelings. So she just shrugged. "I don't know …"

"It was a nice Christmas," Mom continued scrubbing out the sink. "But we did the same things as always. Tia Maria made her same Christmas empanadas, we sang the same songs, you and your brothers and cousins did the same Posadas. Pedro put the baby Jesus in the same manger, and we had a piñata — all just the same as always. So tell me, mija, what made this Christmas your favorite?"

"I just mean that *everything* has been so great this year, Mom. Christmas with the family was really good. But I was also thinking how this is our first Christmas living here in Boscoe Bay, and it's my first Christmas in middle school. And how it's been fun doing things with my friends. Like being in the Christmas parade and our Christmas party in the clubhouse …"

"Oh …" Mom nodded as if taking this in.

"But Christmas with family was great too," Carlie said quickly.

"And I suppose you're looking forward to the big snow trip with your friends?"

"Well, yeah …" Carlie smiled sheepishly. Okay, so Mom had hit the nail right on the head. "That's going to be pretty cool too."

But now Mom's brow creased with worry. "Oh, mija, you must promise to be very careful up there. Tia Maria reminded me that she sprained her ankle on a ski trip in high school. We don't want you getting hurt or breaking anything."

"Don't worry, Mama. I'll be careful."

Mom nodded, but still didn't look too convinced. "And your friend Emily … does she get to go on the snow trip too?"

"Yes, Mama." Carlie carefully swept the small pile of dirt into the dustpan. She knew her parents had been pretty upset over the recent situation with Emily and her family. They hadn't said much to Carlie, but she'd overheard them discussing concerns about Emily's dad and whether or not the neighborhood was safe with a man like that in town. Although Carlie was fairly certain he was still safely locked up in jail after breaking and entering and threatening to kidnap his family. Even so, Carlie had heard her father say that he was going to be on a special lookout … just in case the creep showed up again. For that matter, the whole neighborhood would be watching for him. But Carlie thought that was probably a good thing. No one wanted anything bad to happen to Emily or her family.

"And Emily's mother isn't … well, she's not worried at all?"

"I think her mom is just thankful that they got back home in time for Christmas," she said carefully. Carlie knew that it was always best not to worry her mother. For some reason Mom worried a lot. She worried about other people's problems and worried about her house not being clean enough. Carlie mostly didn't get it. But that was her mom. Just then Carlie heard her little brother Pedro screaming like he'd been hurt — probably pushed down by four-year-old Michael again.

"There they go again," said Mom.

"I can finish up in here," Carlie said quickly, "if you want to go check on the boys."

"Thanks, mija," Her mom peeled off the rubber gloves and handed them to Carlie. "What would I do without my girl?"

Carlie didn't answer that one, but she had a pretty good idea of what her mom would do without her. She'd probably pull out her hair and scream so loudly that Mr. Greeley would come running with his shotgun. Carlie knew that Pedro and Michael pushed Mom's patience to the max, but being the older sister of those wild little boys was no picnic for Carlie either. And even though Mom paid her for babysitting — *sometimes* anyway — Carlie could hardly wait to escape her rowdy brothers for three precious days.

She sighed as she washed the stovetop. In her mind's eye she could see the pristine mountain, not so different from the photo on the brochure that Morgan had first shown them. And Carlie could imagine the white snow and the peaceful calm of being outside. Better yet would be hanging with her friends. But the best part of all would be not having to wipe a runny nose or scrub a sticky face or tell a screaming boy to "just be quiet!" It would be so awesome to be at the ski lodge, hanging with her best friends and no little brothers. It sounded like heaven to her.

In fact, that's what today's "meeting" was about. The girls were gathering at the clubhouse to try on ski clothes and pack and plan for the trip. Fortunately, Chelsea had lots of snow clothing to share with the others. She had wanted them to come up to her big fancy house to try things on, but Emily had talked her into coming to the clubhouse instead. And Carlie had been glad to hear that. In Carlie's mind, the clubhouse was their own special place. Just because Chelsea didn't live in Harbor View shouldn't give her the right to try to change things. Sometimes Carlie felt like the original four girls — Morgan, Emily, Amy, and she had to stand their ground with Chelsea. But she knew that wasn't a very good attitude. And, really, most of the time she liked Chelsea.

As Carlie cleaned, she planned what she might take on the ski trip. Unfortunately, she didn't have much in the way of ski clothes. Although her aunt and uncle had gotten her a pale blue belted parka for Christmas, and she couldn't wait to show it to her friends. Really, this had been an awesome Christmas break so far. And it was only going to get better.

As she scrubbed the bathtub, tossing her brothers' tubby toys into the mesh bag, she mentally checked off what she might pack for the ski trip. Nothing fancy, of course, just some sweatshirts and her favorite jeans and maybe her Tommy Hilfiger warm-ups. Carlie frowned as she remembered how she'd been influenced by Chelsea last fall, being talked into spending way too much money for certain items of clothing. Carlie wasn't into that anymore. Wasting money on designer labels just seemed plain stupid now. Of course, she wouldn't say that to Chelsea.

Finally, it was nearly two, and Carlie was done with the bathroom that she shared with her brothers. Sure, it might not be as perfect as Mom would like — since Mom was, after all, the Queen of Clean — but it was close. And, at least, it smelled good now. That was challenge enough with her two little brothers and their messy habits. As she came out in the hallway, she noticed that the house had gotten nice and quiet, and Carlie suspected her brothers were already down for their naps. So she went to her room and threw some things in her duffle bag to take to the clubhouse. It seemed sort of dumb now, but Chelsea had insisted that they all bring to the clubhouse what they intended to take on the ski trip. She said this was going to be a packing party. The best part was that she was bringing refreshments.

"Running away from home?" asked Mom when Carlie nearly ran into her in the hallway.

"No." Carlie grinned sheepishly. "It's our packing party. Remember, I told you about —"

"Yes, I remember." Mom nodded. "Just teasing.

"Well, it is kind of silly ... but Chelsea is the fashion expert, you know, and she wants us to look our best."

"Nothing wrong with that," said Mom. "I always want my family to look nice." She ran her hand over Carlie's shoulder-length dark curls. "And I like my girl to brush her hair and —"

"I know, Mama." Carlie glanced at the clock. "But I'm already running late."

"Okay, have fun."

Carlie quietly closed the door behind her and slung the strap of her duffle bag over her shoulder. It felt so good to be outside. Even with the damp chill and the brisk breeze, Carlie would much rather be out here than in a stuffy house. She breathed deeply, letting the sea-scented air fill her lungs and holding it a long time before exhaling. Some people, like Mom, didn't like the smell of the ocean. Mom often said that it smelled dirty — like rotten fish and old seaweed — but Carlie thought it smelled full of life. In fact, Carlie sometimes thought she might like to be a marine biologist. Either that or she'd like to be a landscape designer or maybe work in forestry. Whatever Carlie did, she knew it would be an outside job — and she would never have to comb her hair if she didn't want to, and she could get her hands just as dirty as she pleased.

"Hey, Carlie," called Amy Ngo as she jogged to catch up with her. Like Carlie, she was lugging a bag. "You're late."

"Just a few minutes," said Carlie. "But I'm surprised *you're* late." She grinned down at her petite friend. "Little Miss *I Hate to be Late*."

"Yes, well, I had to work lunch at the restaurant today. My sister An took off without telling anyone."

"Where'd she go?" Carlie was curious. Of all of Amy's older siblings, Carlie liked An the best.

"No one knows," said Amy mysteriously. "She disappeared last night after work and never came home."

Carlie blinked. "Are your parents freaking?"

"A little. But, as you know, An is an adult — she's twenty-seven. I guess if she wants to take off, she should be able to."

"But what if something's wrong?"

Amy giggled. "Well, Ly is saying that An probably eloped with her new boyfriend."

"Eloped?"

Amy nodded with a sly grin. "But I don't think so."

"And you're not worried?"

"An has a good head on her shoulders."

"Yes," agreed Carlie. "But I hope she's okay."

"She's just teaching Ly a lesson," said Amy as they reached the clubhouse, which they'd converted from an old hippie bus. "They got into a big fight at the restaurant yesterday."

"Well," said Carlie as she opened the door. "That explains everything."

"Hey, it's about time," called out Chelsea as the two of them entered the bus. Carlie was glad to see that the others were already there. And she took in another deep breath as she closed the door behind her. Like the sea air, Carlie liked the smell of their old clubhouse too. Oh, she was sure that her mother would not approve. She would probably think it smelled musty and in need of a good cleaning. But Carlie always thought the clubhouse smelled more like an adventure about to begin. And usually that was the case.

A New Series from Faithgirlz!

Meet Morgan, Amy, Carlie, and Emily. They all live in the trailer park at 622 Harbor View in tiny Boscoe Bay, Oregon. Proximity made them friends, but a desire to make the world a better place—and a willingness to work at it—keeps them together.

Project: Girl Power

Book One • Softcover • ISBN 0-310-71186-X

After a face-off with a group of bullies, Morgan, Amy, Carlie, and Emily decide to walk to and from school together. There's safety in numbers. Then the girls notice how ugly their mobile home park looks. With help from other people in the park, they beautify Harbor View, which brings surprising consequences.

Project: Mystery Bus

Book Two • Softcover • ISBN 0-310-71187-8

The girls of 622 Harbor View begin summer by working to clean and restore their bus to use as a clubhouse. As they work on the bus, they discover clues that suggest someone who lived in the bus during the late '70s had a mysterious past and is somehow connected with grumpy Mr. Greeley, the manager.

Project: Rescue Chelsea

Book Three • Softcover • ISBN 0-310-71188-6

Carlie makes a new friend. Chelsea Landers lives in a mansion and isn't always very kind. Carlie would like a best friend, but will Chelsea fit in with her other friends? When Carlie is betrayed by Chelsea, she learns how much she appreciates her friends in the Rainbow Club. This is a story about forgiveness and accepting differences.

Project: Take Charge

Book Four • Softcover • ISBN 0-310-71189-4

The girls of 622 Harbor View find out their town's only city park has been vandalized and may soon be turned into a parking lot. They group together to save their beloved park and soon meet an elderly woman with the power to help their cause, or stop it before it even starts. But will they be able to convince her to help before it's too late?

Project: Raising Faith

Book Five • Softcover • ISBN 0-310-71349-8

When the girls set out to raise the money to go on a three-day ski trip with the church youth group, Morgan is confident that God will provide the funds. But while everyone else finds a way to afford the trip, Morgan's plans are derailed by her grandmother's illness, school, Christmas activities, even jealousy ... and when Grandma suffers a heart attack, Morgan's faith is severely tested. Will God provide what's really important?

Project: Run Away

Book Six • Softcover • ISBN 0-310-71350-1

Shortly before Christmas, Emily's family must flee when her abusive father uncovers them in Boscoe Bay. But Emily's friends rally to help get them safely back home where Emily discovers that forgiveness doesn't always come easily.

Available now at your local bookstore! Visit www.faithgirlz.com

Faithgirlz! is based on 2 Corinthians 4:18—So we fix our eyes not on what is seen, but on what is unseen. For what is seen is temporary, but what is unseen is eternal (NIV) — and helps girls find the beauty of believing.

We want to hear from you. Please send your comments about this book to us in care of zreview@zondervan.com. Thank you.

ZONDERVAN.com/
AUTHORTRACKER
follow your favorite authors